IAN BILLINGS'
LOST PROPERTY

Poems! Stories! jokes! Cheese!
and lots of silliness by
ian Billings
with cartoons by Hunt Emerson.

IAN BILLINGS' LOST PROPERTY

Subject to condition

IAN BILLINGS' LOST PROPERTY
© Ian Billings 2015
Cover and illustrations by Hunt Emerson.
Published by Tiddley Pom 2015.
The Coach House,
Tettenhall,
West Midlands.

iNTRODUCTiON

Welcome to this book. You will soon be overwhelmed by the wonderful magnificence and astounding beauty of the book and, like me, you will soon realise it is the greatest ever written in any language, anywhere in the universe. Every word of this book has taken years to create, mould and imbed on the page. It is without doubt the finest piece of writing ever written ever, ever, ever. So there. If I was reviewing this book on Amazon I'd give it a million, million stars...

STOP, STOP, STOP! That's the wrong introduction. This is the correct introduction:

Welcome to "How to Cook a Wardrobe". First you need to find a really fresh wardrobe. It doesn't matter how many doors. Then you fillet the shelves and peel off the varnish. Don't throw away the varnish. You will need it later for the sauce. Then place a pan on the cooker. It needs to be a really big pan. Probably about two metres by three metres. You can buy these pans by sending £100,000 to my website www.howtogetmoneyfromstupidreaders.com then wait two years...

STOP, STOP, STOP. That's the wrong introduction, too. This is the correct introduction:

Hello,

Welcome to my book. I hope you like it. It's a bit silly.

Ian Billings

CONTENTS

JACK HORNER R.S.i.- RHYME SQUAD iNVESTiGATiONS

Episode One –
Humpty Dumpty: was he pushed or did he fall?

My name's Horner, Jack Horner, Lieutenant Detective Jack Horner of the Once Upon a Time Town Special Investigation Unit – the Rhyme Squad.

Every 60 seconds in this town a rhyme is committed. Sometimes it's a little minor verse, sometimes a haiku, sometimes a complete sonnet is pulled off. And it's my job to see it doesn't happen. I was driving my car down Ding Dong Dell thinking about some of the rhymes I'd solved in the past month.

Little Miss Muffet – mugged by a spider,
Tom, Tom the Piper's son – pig rustling, managed to avoid capture and away he did run.
Wee Willie Winkie – usual crime.

All was quiet in Once Upon a Time Town – too quiet.
When I arrived at the precinct a beautiful young dame with a bonnet and shepherd's crook was waiting at my desk.
"I lost my sheep!"
"What's your name, ma'am?"
"Peep."
"First name?"
"Bo!"
"Could you describe your sheep?"
"It's fleece was white as... white as..."
"Snow, ma'am?"
"Yeah!"

1

"We get a lot of lost sheep."

Suddenly the phone rang. Seems a new rhyme had been committed. It was an IC1, male, Caucasian, completely bald, 850 pounds by the name of H. Dumpty was broken in a thousand pieces at the bottom of the wall. My job was to find out who pushed him. As I rushed from the station I heard a voice - "What about my sheep?"

At the scene of the rhyme squad cars had pulled up by the wall and crowds of fairy tale folk were being held back. A riot officer was calling through a megaphone -
"Move away from the egg shell! Move away from the egg shell! Nothing to see here!"
I grabbed a glass of milk, a hot cross bun and went in.

It was a horrible sight – it was a yolk bath! Egg shell every where! In the corner of the crowd I saw an old informant of mine, his name was Baa Baa.
"Hi, Baa-baa! Got any wool on you?"
"I don't do wool no more, Mr. Horner."
"Know anything about this rhyme?"
"That kinda information'll cost you Mr. Horner."
"How much?"
"Half a pound of tuppenny rice, half a pound of treacle."
I paid him and he drew me aside.
"This ain't Humpty Dumpty, Mr. Horner. I saw it all with my own eyes. Dumpty stole eggs from the Ugly Duckling and Goosey-Goosey Gander and he smashed them on the ground himself."
"But why?"
"For the insurance! He insured his life for 1,000,000 gold coins. All he has to do is collect the insurance money and he'll be living happily ever after."

At that point there was a noise at the back of the crowd and a character elbowed his way through. Big guy about 850 pounds, IC1,male, Caucasian but with a full head of hair.

"My poor brother, Humpty, what has happened to you?"
"Who are you?" I asked.
"I am Humpty Dumpty's brother."
"And what's your name?"
"My name?"
"Yep."
"Erm… My name is… Flumpty Dumpty."

Suddenly it all became clear I grabbed at his hair, gave it a tug and it came away in my hand. There was a gasp from the crowd – "Hey diddle diddle!" they went. He was completely bald.

"You are Humpty Dumpty – this is just an insurance scam. I'll see you get 6 months hard labour with the Grand Old Duke of York. He'll march to the top of the hill and he'll march back again!"
"Six months – I'll be passed my sell by date!" he squealed.
"Hey, hey, hey – if you can't do the time don't do the rhyme! Take him away, boys!"

That night Once Upon a Time Town was quiet again – all that could be heard was the sound of happy nursery rhyme folk going about their business and the distant sound of weasels going pop. I returned to my office and wrote up my report :

Detective Jack Horner sat in a corner
eating an apple pie.
I stuck in my thumb
and pulled out a plum
and thought, "I'm a great private eye!"

SLiME TRiALS

The Snail Three-Yard Dash was run in a flash,
Those snails have so much power.
Now they had to be told who had won the snail gold
After speeding at 3 yards an hour.

Who was it who won at the end of the run?
Who had the best snaily motion?
The judge, in a stir, said, "It was all a blur!"
His voice was full of emotion.

Snails started to moan, jeer, sneer, gripe and groan.
It was causing a snaily commotion.
The judge said, at last, "But it all happened so fast!
Let's watch it again in slow motion!"

INSECT-A-SIDE FOOTBALL

The Earwig Match was underway
What a fine six-legged display!
But hear the crowd groan and growl
When Earwig One commits a foul
The Earwig ref does not think hard,
before showing him the earwig card.

An earwig substitute is chosen,
sitting on the bench shocked and frozen.
He'd never played a big match before
Could he do it? Could he score?
He couldn't tell. He didn't know.
He only knew his number – 0!

He was worried, cos here's the thing,
Before he'd only played in wing!
Onto the pitch he comes bounding,
Feeling fit, his heart is pounding.
Then a chant sets his heart aglow,
They're calling his name - "Earwig O, Earwig O, Earwig O!"

THE SEAL

Chocolate animal biscuits.
I adore them – there's
Giraffes, lions, tigers,
Penguins and there's bears.

The supermarket was beckoning me,
So I bought a pack today.
But suddenly I stopped and stared
Whilst on my way to pay.

I read the packet carefully,
I'm always quite precise.
It was then I saw a notice
That really caught my eyes.

I hurried down the shopping aisle.
Packet clutched in hand.
I couldn't stop or wait a while
To enjoy my favourite brand.

But the notice had upset me,
I had to know the truth.
I waited for the manager
to come out of his booth.

I shouted at the manager
(Now I wish I hadn't spoken)
"Is it true I can't eat this food -
if the seal is broken?"

SPROUT

"What's it all about?"
thought the lonely little sprout,
sitting on the canteen tray.

"I wonder what the use is
sitting in my juices,
hoping to be whisked away."

"I wish I were a chip,
covered all in dip
not just cold and old debris."

But all that grease
Makes kids obsese
I'm glad I'm just little old me.

ON TELLY LATER TONIGHT

On telly later tonight,
There's plenty of stuff to delight.
Two dogs in pyjamas,
whilst eating bananas
And a bishop flying a kite.

There's a partly political broadcast
And a cat with the weather forecast,
A ship wrapped in foil
The queen eating soil,
And a musical Elastoplast.

At ten a programme on warts.
Then a rabbit shares his thoughts.
On the state of the world,
Why his lettuce has curled
And how good he looks in pink shorts.

We've a programme on jumping in puddles,
And some aardvarks sitting in huddles
Cookery, too.
A man eats his shoe.
And the Prime Minister appeals for more cuddles

There's dribbling for the beginner,
A postman sits in his dinner,
Two chat show hosts,
Climb up some posts
And a ferret says both are the winner.

But it's all a lie you see
None of it's on TV.
It's just been invented
By an announcer, demented.
You really must excuse,
I did it to amuse.
I'm easily bored
I should be ignored
Sorry about that – here's the news.

DAME PEGGIE SLOPS AND
HER HAUNTED WOODEN LEG

This was the Cluttered Plughole – and it lived up to its name. It was a tatty tavern that was home from home to a fearsome fleet of plucky pirates. All shapes and sizes were washed up in the Cluttered Plughole, pirates from across the globe, pirates from across the street, each with a salty tale to tell of adventures at sea.

Mr. Blackbarrel, the musician, was hunched over the grotty grand piano and his spindly fingers poked the battered keys like tongs poking a fire. As he poked out a sea-shanty, snatches of conversations could be heard.
"My head was stuck in that cannon for a week..."
"Then I grabbed him by the ears and flung him overboard..."

"I didn't know he had a glass-eye until it came out in the conversation…"
"Cheese and onion crisps, please!"

The last sound came from a voice that belonged to a mouth which was owned by a face which had once been very familiar in these parts.

"Dame Peggie Slops!" croaked the barman, unable to believe what he was seeing. A few heads turned as he croaked his croak. "Dame Peggie Slops!" he cried. "There she blows! The finest pirate ever to nick a clipper out of Portsmouth. Tales of the derring-do she's dared do are part of the folk-lore hereabouts!" Mr. Blackbarrel battered a hearty tune from the piano in celebration as the barman filled a frothy tankard for their star guest. He leaned across the wet bar and said, "So, Dame Peggie, what brings you back?"

Dame Peggie Slops was a sprightly pirate. Her long white hair tresselled down her back and she had the complexion of someone half her age. She was seventy-two and still had all her own teeth – in a jar by her bed. She slipped the crisps from the barman's grasp and her twinkling eyes gave him a naughty wink as she slid away.

The barman sighed as she went, but then he noticed Dame Peggie was limping. She never used to limp, he thought as he turned to the next customer.

In a quiet corner of the tavern sat a small man with a hat too large for his head and a smile too wide for his face. The smile widened as Dame Peggie limped towards him.
Was this the man she was looking for?

"Would you like a cheese and onion crisp?" she asked, opening the packet and offering its contents. This was a pre-arranged code - if he gave the correct answer she would know he was the man.

"Thank you," he said, "but I only eat salt and vinegar."

Dame Peggie crunched the packet, threw it aside and slid into the seat next to him. That was the correct answer. "Doctor Residue?" she asked.

The man lifted his hat and almost took off his fake wig, too.

"The same!" he said, and the smile slithered across his face. "So you'd like a wooden leg, would you?"

Dame Peggie hushed him and explained in a low voice.

"I have tangled with the vilest villains afloat and have never had a scar, a bruise or even a graze! But three months ago I encountered a pack of the most vicious penguins you could imagine and, well…" She grimaced at the memory. "I will not go into too much detail, but where I once had two legs I now only have one."

Doctor Residue scanned the chattering masses of the tavern and then bent down under the table. He re-emerged clutching a large leather suitcase with big brass clasps, which, like his face, had not been cleaned for a very long time. He clicked the clasps and the lid popped open.

He turned the case just enough for Dame Peggie to see its contents, without revealing them to the pub.

The old sea-saltress gasped. Inside the suitcase, nestling amongst plush red velvet, were five wooden legs.

"This is just what I need," whispered Dame Peggie.

"But which will you choose?" asked the Doctor.

She ran her hand over the legs and slowly began making her choice. Her finger stopped on one specimen. It was a fine, cedarwood leg, with a strong ankle, a firm calf and perfectly trimmed toenails.

"This one!" she announced.

Doctor Residue giggled and said, "A wise choice, my lady, only one previous owner. And she only used it for going to the shops on a Sunday."

He slipped the leg from the case, wrapped it in brown paper and handed it over.

Dame Peggie hid it in the folds of her dress and smiled at the Doctor.

"And my money?"

Dame Peggie produced a bag of gold coins from another fold and slid it across the table. They nodded at each other and both disappeared into the crowd.

The deed was done, the agreement was sealed and the story had begun.

Dame Peggie scurried away into the darkest darkness of the night. Clutched under her grateful arm was the leg she had yearned for. That night she would practise her fox trot, her tango and her cha-cha like there was no tomorrow. But there was a tomorrow and it would be the day of the Pirates' Ball. Dame Peggie was determined to be the finest dancer there – and with her brand new leg, how could she fail?

✳✳✳

Two tankards clinked together, some froth was slopped and two voices giggled, cackled and guffawed in that order.

Doctor Residue was talking proudly and loudly to his friend, "Admiral" Colin Blotch, a small man in a small uniform with a small brain. The so-called Admiral had been hit on the head by a cannon ball years before. Now he could not even tie his shoelaces without a chart. He stared at the tankard and tried to remember what to do with it.

Doctor Residue swallowed a hearty mouthful and Colin copied. "See, that leg has a history. That leg was not always a leg. That leg was made from a truncheon, once owned by Captain Gruff McHanley, the famous press-ganger. For years he stalked the streets of Portsmouth finding innocent young men and forcing them into a lifetime at sea! You heard of him?" asked the doctor.

Colin thought long and hard about the question and finally said, "No."

Mr. Blackbarrel was fighting a losing battle with his piano as the doctor embarked on the last leg of his tale.

"It is said the ghost of old McHanley still haunts the truncheon – the same truncheon I made into a leg and sold to Dame Peggie Slops." He giggled. Colin giggled, too.

"It is also said that when ever McHanley heard a certain sound he went into a mad frenzy of head hitting, attacking people from here to the Thames."

Colin slurped a final gob of froth from his tankard and said, "What sort of certain sounds?"

Suddenly, Mr.Blackbarrel had his groaning piano under control and was beating out a tune which was jolly and jaunty and jiggy. He launched into a merry dance tune loved by the folk of the Cluttered Plughole. A huge cheer went up drowning out Doctor Residue's final words.

"Music! Dance music!"

✳✳✳

That night the Cluttered Plughole was more cluttered than ever before. Word had spread, sentences had seeped and whole paragraphs had leaked: this was the night of the Pirates' Ball.

The walls were festooned with bunting and the flags of all nations. A fine feast lay across the longest table in the tavern – pilchard trifle, prawn ice cream, whale-tail on toast and octopus dippers for the kids.

Mr. Blackbarrel had dusted off his silver bow tie for the evening and was tinkling away in the corner. The piano had been tuned so if the music sounded awful only his fingers could now be blamed. The party was in full swing and the roar of the crowd was deafening; everyone was having the jolliest of jolly times. (Everyone except one small woman by the name of Mary Celeste, who was banging her empty tankard on the bar trying – and failing – to attract the barman's attention. She was getting very annoyed.)

Already folks had entered the dancing contest. Claude and Maude D'courcy had wowed the audience with their triple fandango and Betty Ricketts had performed a sizzling break dance in which she'd broken a lot of things – a fingernail, a jug of lemonade and the record for oddest dance of the competition.
Each contestant was judged by a po-faced pirate, Mrs J.T. Butterbox . She had a chalk board on which she scribbled marks out of ten. So far, she looked bored as a plank.

"Ladles and diddle-men," Mr.Blackbarrel announced eventually, "My have I you untension? Is there any more dancering people wishing to sally forth on the dance flow and do us a diddling dance?"
Faces looked at faces which looked at faces which looked at faces. Everyone who wished to dance had, it seemed, danced.
"Very welly, then! I shall ask the budgie to…"
"Wait!"
A hooded figure which had silently appeared in the corner whisked off its hood and revealed itself to be -
"Dame Peggie Slops!" croaked the barman. "She always knows how to make an entrance!"
The light tinkled off her tiara. Her newly polished teeth gleamed in her mouth. Her dress trickled with jewellery. She struck a pose in the centre of the room and waited.

Mr Blackbarrel coughed. He leaned forward, shielding his eyes from the glittering costume and said, "I doughnut have any music!"

The beer tap dripped in expectation. Everyone waited. Dame Peggie was frozen in the glare of every eye in the room.

The silence was broken by a small woman banging her tankard on the bar. It was Mary Celeste again.

"Beer!" she shrieked.

Ambrose Click, the oldest barman this side of the Nile, ambled over and held his hand to his ear.

"Eh?"

"I want a can of beer to take away!"

"Eh?" he said again.

She suddenly breathed deeply and bellowed loudly,

"Can! Can!"

"Oh, a cancan!" said Mr. Blackbarrel, leaping back on his stool and grabbing the piano like it was about to escape. He began belting out the tune to the best of his abilities.

Dame Peggie Slops stood as still as a clipper without a whiff of wind. This was not the music she had rehearsed to. What was she to do? She looked at the expectant faces and decided to give it a go.

Dame Peggie spun and span and twirled and turned. She dipped and doffed, tangoed, foxtrotted and cha-cha-chaed. All to the sound of the cancan! The amazed eyes of the Cluttered Plugholers widened with each dazzling step.

Mrs J.T. Butterbox began muttering to herself and even smiled.

Then things started to go wrong.

"Ooooooooooooooooooooooooooooooooooooooooooooo!!!!"

It was a moaning groan! No one seemed to know where it was coming from, but everyone could hear it. Then Dame Peggie gasped as she felt her wooden leg twitching under her dress. Suddenly, without warning, it performed a dance move she had not rehearsed. Except it wasn't a dance move. The wooden leg was actually dragging Dame Peggie towards Mrs. Butterbox.

Step by step she moved closer, step by step she tried to resist. The spectators all held their breath as Dame Peggie was dragged closer and closer to the judge. No one realised that the music was causing the chaos and Mr. Blackbarrel, thinking he could quell the madness, played even louder.

The hopping Dame Peggie was led along until the leg was in clouting distance of the judge. It appeared from under Dame Peggie's beautiful white dress, like a cannon raising up and spotting its target. And its target was the Mrs. Butterbox.

With one swift swat the leg swiped – and missed! Mrs. Butterbox whooped and whimpered and ran for the door.
The leg scanned the silent room and poor Dame Peggie pivoted on the spot. It was looking for another victim and soon located Mr. Blackbarrel. Once again, poor Dame Peggie was dragged along, this time towards the gulping musician. By now she had come to her senses and shouted, "Pull it off! Pull it off!" But the audience hadn't come to its senses and didn't know what to pull off.

The leg clunked towards the stage.
Mr. Blackbarrel could do nothing except play louder and louder.
The leg got closer and closer.
It dragged Dame Peggie up the steps, onto the stage and across to Mr. Blackbarrel. Inches away from the musician's sweating head, it hovered in front of his crossed eyes.

Suddenly Mr. Blackbarrel grabbed the wooden leg, placed it under his arm and swirled Dame Peggie Slops onto the dance floor. They stood silently, the appendage finally stilled by the lack of music. The gawping eyes of the Cluttered Plugholers stared without blinking for second after second after second. The barman, a quick-thinking fellow, whipped from beneath the bar a small, portable gramophone player. A huge brass horn protruded from the top and a handle dangled from the side. He slid it across the damp bar to Mary Celeste. She stared at it in bewilderment and said, "Is this a wind-up?"

"Yes!" hissed the barman. "Turn the handle!"

And she did and from the brass horn pumped a joyful dance tune which no one's feet could resist. Dame Peggie and her new partner started tapping theirs, then slapped their hands and finally launched into a full-flung dance routine. They ducked and dived and span and spun. It was the perfect dance routine – Dame Peggie performed the steps she had rehearsed and Mr. Blackbarrel kept her haunted leg under control.

"Oooooooooooooooooooooh!" said the leg, starting to sound a little confused.

As the dance finished, the crowd roared its approval and Dame Peggie finally removed her leg. All three took a bow.

"Oooooooooooooooooooooh!" As the leg started to twitch and tremble once more, Mr. Blackbarrel snatched it and hurled it through the tavern window. All fell silent in the room until the distant splash of the plopping leg was heard – at which point a huge cheer went up!

The barman climbed up onto his bar and declared to the merry masses, "Dame Peggie Slops, ladies and gentlemen. I think you will agree with me when I say that was the finest performance ever seen on these shores!" He started to clap and one by one all the Plugholers joined in and the clapping became cheering and the cheering became stomping. And in the midst of the clapping, cheering and stomping the barman hopped over to the judge's empty chair and picked up the first prize: a bright, shiny golden cup on which was printed

For the Finest Sea-Legs on Dry Land

He presented the cup to Dame Peggie Slops, who was breathless, gobsmacked and a little confused. But she gracefully received the award and agreed to pose for an oil-painting for the local gallery. She even slipped her arm around Mr. Blackbarrel.

The rest of the evening was spent in a rollicking, jollisome swirl of fun and frolics. Each and every pirate would one day tell of the time they witnessed the dance of Dame Peggie Slops and her Haunted Wooden Leg.

MRS. MALCOLM

Mrs. Malcolm had a theory
On how to keep her pupils cheery.
She gave them custard, jam and honey
And bribed each one with eggs (quite runny)
To keep them happy she gave them sweets,
"There's a prize for everyone who cheats!
For copying there's a giant cake –
And a carrot for every rule you break!
For missing school I'll give a toffee -
 and for a mummy a jar of coffee."

Mrs. Malcolm had a letter
Telling her to do much better.
Then she had to see the Head –
Whom most approached with fear and dread.
But Mrs. Malcolm knocked the door
And gaily skipped across the floor.
He told her, as his face turned green
"You're worst teacher I've ever seen.
The way you teach makes me wail –
Each and every child will fail!"
A look of joy then crossed her eyes
And she simply said, "So where's my prize?"

It really was an awful to do -
But don't you wish Mrs. Malcolm taught you?

BEWARE! TAKE CARE!

Our school caretaker, Mr. Mole
Didn't take care - so he fell in a hole.

When your job's about taking care,
If there's a hole in the ground you should beware.

(PS – Don't worry about the hole in the ground – the police are looking into it.)

THE MONSTER IN THE HALLWAY

Here it bursts right through the door,
Hear it snarling, hear it roar.
Scowling, frowning, yelling, yawning.
A scary sight on Monday morning.

It sniffs the air, its teeth go crunch
It knows there's ravioli for lunch.
It walks the hall stalking prey
wishing for an indoor play.

"The monsters loose inside the school!",
Watch them scatter through the drool.
Trying to avoid detection,
They hide themselves inside reception.

It licks the ground where a child fell
Then hisses at the morning bell.
It knows the children are all trembling
As in the hall they start assembling.

It follows them in, running wild,
Clawing at each frightened child
Chasing children, gnawing bones -
we simply call her Mrs. Jones.

PUNK-TUATION!

Why can't we hear all the commas?
Why is a fullstop quite mute?
What noise does a ! make?
This really doesn't compute.

When you read a good piece of writing,
You listen for every word –
But I have a proclamation -
It's time punctuation was heard!

Let's give voice to a colon
Let's make a noise for a stop.
An apostrophe yearns for a yelling.
Let's make literacy hop!

Dashes, hashes, forward-slashes,
Hyphens could go twang,
Apostrophes could yodel
And asterisks go clang!

Ber-doing go a couple of brackets,
Kerrang go quotation marks,
@ signs probably tinkle
Sound bites as bad as their barks.

History will show we're not stupid
We've invented a brand new art
Ellipsis could sound like sneezes
And a full stop could sound like a –

Part of the new generation
Of people speaking this way.
Make punctuation noisy.
Run out and try it today!

MY NOSE
(A poem not to be sniffed at)

I've decided to sell my nose
It doesn't go well with these clothes
I need something more trendy
and perhaps a bit bendy
that doesn't snore when I doze.

So then came the great day
I posted my nose on Ebay
I had 2000 hits
I was thrilled to bits,
but none of them wanted to pay.

SPELLINK

Spellink mistooks are quite bad
They drive your toocher mad
So poofread your prose
and then who nose?
Your toocher may start feeling glad!

WHEN SANTA TURNS BAD

The best time of year at school is Xmas. It's great. The school nativity with all the shepherds with tea towels on their heads – and the Christmas Tree is in the corner of the hall, slightly depressed, saying :

"Why am I always in a bucket? I'm always in a bucket - I'll be standing here for hours now – I'll get pins and needles – oh, I've already got needles. Leave my baubles alone – go on shooo! Look, at that! He ran off with my bauble! Oh, if it wasn't for this bucket! I got a fairy on my head. "

Everyone's excited because the moment you've all been waiting for arrives –

"Santa's here! Santa's here!" they all chant, and into the school hall walks Santa, the main man, trying to be trendy...

"Yo –kiddies!" he says, "I am Santa. Get down - the chimney!"

Then everyone gets a chance to tell him what you want for Xmas. One says, "Can I have a pebble? No, no, no, no - wait a minute... Yeah, a pebble!"

Then there's more requests –

"I wanna yo-yo, not a yo yo, a yo-yo!"

"I wanna an orange Rubik's cube!"

"I wanna, I wanna, I wanna, I wanna, I wanna!!!!!"

Meanwhile at the North Pole – where the snow is like a pizza – deep-pan, crisp and even – there's a little grotto, tinkling with lanterns, a rosy glow of candlelight at the window – it's Santa's Grotto - But Mr. Pootle, the Head of Distribution, is not very happy!

"I'm not very happy!" he says – see I told you - "The elves they just walked out! How can I run a high speed distribution system without elves? Maybe I was too harsh on them. Maybe I shouldn't have used the whip. No toy, no joy! Stupid elves. Oh, ding-dong-ding. (That's elf rude words.) I gotta tell the big guy in red. Santa Claus, Kris Kringle, Pappy Happy Holidays. No, won't be a Happy Pappy for very long!"
He goes over to Santa's door and knock, knock, knocks on it.
"Knock, knock, knock - Ho, ho, ho!" he shouts, brightly.
"Ho, ho and ho!" says Santa's voice from inside.
"I got something to tell you." says Mr. Pootle putting his head round the door.
"Just look what I got" says Santa indicating the mobile phone in his hand, "My one billionenth text message…Dear Santa…"
"I really gotta tell you…" interrupts Mr. Pootle
"…Please give me – there's a list here as long as my beard…Want, want, want… millions of requests. Listen to this – a Playdoh Playstation? – What's that? A Barbie wii? A My Little Pony Pet Cemetary– what's that? Am I getting too old for this? Extreme Tiddleywinks? It's not easy being Santa - 24 hours to deliver 370 million presents – that's 800 visits a second. 1/800th of a second to park up, deliver, climb down some pretty disgusting chimneys – and if I ever see another mince pie…And, you know, in all that time. In all those years of dragging sacks of presents – in all that time…. Nobody ever asked me what I wanted."
Mr. Pootle tried to interrupt again.
"You know what I want – a new hip! What is it?"

"Now, listen, Santa, I gotta tell you something. And you must promise not to get upset..."

"What's happened?"
"The elves walked out!"
"The elves walked out?"yells Santa.
"Well, they kinda skipped – but that's elves!"
"The elves walked out - are you pulling my cracker?"
"Every single elf."
"What am I gonna do? Elvish has left the building...."
"370 million children demanding presents! 350 years at the North Pole we never had a workers' strike. What am I gonna do, what am I gonna dooooooooooooo?"
"Okay, Santa, chill!"
"350 years at the North Pole – I know how to chill!"he bellows
"Somebody's not in touch with their inner pixie."
"370 million presents to deliver, a bad back and no elves! This is the icing on the Xmas cake! That's it! I've had up to here with those little people – elves, children, reindeer! I can't take it anymore! From now on no more Mr.Nice Guy. Ha! Saddle up Randolph the Reindeer...Plug in the Santa Nav! –"
And soon they're away and all you see is Santa's sleigh zigzaging across the stars – "Try a straight line, Randolph!" and the distant sound of the Santa Nav saying, "At Greenland turn right, turn right, turn right..."
"Listen to the Santa Nav, Randolph!"
But what will happen to Santa? What will happen to Randolph?

To be continued....

COLOURS

There's a rumour going round
Colours each have their own sound
I know it's true
Though do you?
But you'll have rainbows in your ears - wait and see

I think the Blue would go, "Boo-Hoo!"
And the Brown would shout out, "Boo!"
And the Purple would simply go, "Wheeeee!"

The Red would shout out, "Grrrr!"
and the Magenta softly purr
And the Yellow would loudly go, "Tee-heee!"

The Jasmin would say, "Wow!"
and the Violet, "Ka-pow!"
I really hope that all of you agree.

Then the Green would go, "Shush!"
at the Orange going, "Whoosh!"
This all makes perfect sense to me.

WHERE DO YOU GET AN IDEA?

Where do you get an idea?
Do they simply go "Pop!" and appear?
Do you rummage around
on the roof, on the ground?
Oh, where do you get an idea?

Where do you get an idea?
Do they simply fall in your ear?
Are they just in your brain?
Or is it a pain?
Oh, where do you get an idea?

Where do you get an idea?
Are they far off or really quite near?
Are they kept in a box?
Or stuffed in your socks?
Oh, where do you get an idea?

Where do you get an idea?
It's really not very clear.
Have you magical powers
Or do you slave for hours?
Oh, where do you get an idea?

Here's where I get my ideas.
It's something I've been doing for years.
I simply pay
and get them all off Ebay.
That's where I get my ideas!

ANT

A colony of fun-loving ants
got an invite to a local bug dance
But then half way through,
screamed, "What shall we all do?
We've all forgotten our pants!"

ALBATROSS

An albatross called Albert Ross
One day was quite at a loss
"It's a shame that my name
is the same name again.
It makes me ever so cross!"

BARN OWL

A very naughty barn owl,
once dressed himself in a towel
But the towel was too hot
for his small birdy bot
And goodness did that owl howl!

BEAR

One day roared a grizzly bear,
"I've come to fill you with fear!"
Now's not the time
to say, "That don't rhyme!"
But to quietly disappear.

COCKROACH

A European cockroach
had a very interesting approach
to attracting a mate
He'd swing from a gate
wearing a huge red broach.

DODO

There once was a small dodo
gorgeous from head to toe
Wouldn't you think
they would not be extinct?
But they are, "Oh, no, oh, no…"

FISH

A chef had a desperate wish
to invent a completely new dish
If you look in the sky
You'll see it go by
"I'm trying frying flying fish!"

FOX

There once was a terrified fox
who was frighten by three mighty crocs
He turned out the winner
by not being their dinner
but hiding in a cardboard box

GECKO

There once was a gecko, gecko,
with a passion for Art Deco Deco
He once built a hall hall
three hundred feet tall tall
Pretty, but, boy, did it echo echo!

GERBIL

There once was sweet gerbil
Whose owners had named him Phil
He ran round his wheel
and said, "I no longer feel
Like a Phil. From now on I'm Jill!"

KANGAROO

There once was kangaroo
who hopped off to Katmandu
He hopped through Nepal
with no problem at all
"There's no end to what I can do!"

LLAMA

There once was a gallant young llama
who dressed in bright, white armour
and when attacked by a tapier
swinging a rapier
took seconds to swiftly disarm her

34

OCTOPUS

There once was an octopus
whose talents I'd like to discuss
She could dance and plate spin,
eat sardines from a tin
and all whilst driving a bus

SALAMANDER

There once was a salamander
whose name happened to be Amanda
If you wanted to view
all her friends in the zoo
you'd have to give her a huge back hander.

SHEEP

Said a sadly depressed little sheep
"I only want to cheep
But then you can't beat
a good sheepy bleat.
Now I'll count people and slip off to sleep."

SWAN

There once was a boring old swan
whose stories went on and on
and on and on
and on and on.
I guess, it takes swan to know one.

VULTURE

There once was a vulgar vulture
who once saw a naked sculpture
"Why do you suppose
they don't wear clothes?
That's really not what I think of as culture!"

TOLLY GRIMPEN'S TALES OF GROT AND HORROR!

Warning!!!
Not to be read by an adult unless accompanied by a child. Contains mild horror and strong gunk throughout

Grotty Contents :

The Gruesome Yarn of the Mummy's Nail Clippings

The Septic Tale of Dr. Jekyll and Mr. Sheen

The Festering Narrative of Uncle Clod

The Bedraggled Story of the Bewitched Teeth

The Rancid Tale of the Child Phenomenon

The Scabby Case of the Ghoulish Gramophone

The Oily Episode of the Pukka Painting

The Smoggy Saga of Jumbo the Ripper

The Cruddy Exploits at Buckett's Hotel

The Gruesome Yarn of the Mummy's Nail Clippings

This is a tale covered in grot from beginning to end. Please wash your hands thoroughly after reading it. It concerns a girl by the name of Florence Gallop, a talkative type with a great deal to talk about. For Florence Gallop was an explorer and, although she was only ten years of age, she had seen more of the world than most grown-ups do in a lifetime. A portrait of her hangs in the Rogues Gallery at the Royal Art Gallery in London. Here it is

At the age of seven, Florence Gallop had conquered Mount Tiddliddloppolos, the lowest mountain in Greece. At eight years she had discovered the Lost Tribe of the Dicki-Whoopers (she discovered them behind her outside lavatory which was a little strange). But by far the weirdest tale in which she partook was the one I am about to relate – the Gruesome Yarn of the Mummy's Nail Clippings.

Many articles have been written about this event and over many

years I collected them together into my grotty scrapbook. This is the first time they have all appear in print and gruesome reading it makes.

The first piece of evidence I lay before your popping eyes is a speech Florence gave in July 1893 to a congregation at St. Paul's Cathedral. This I found in the dusty archives of the Royal Navigational Society - an august institution, which will figure prominently later in our tale. The file had the following words scribbled across it in nervous handwriting –

"Never to be published. Ever. This is due to the awful incidents which have arisen since the authoress put quill to paper. Hide it on the highest shelf."

I carefully opened the file. It was a handwritten scrawl by Florence and in the margins were her own notes. This is what is said –

***

A Speech of Great Scientific Importance to be Heard by Anyone Interested in Important Things by Florence Gallop (aged ten, with her own quill.).

This is a very important speech about nail clippings so jolly well listen closely and I'll tell you how it all happened.

(That got them all interested.)

As you all probably know I am a very important and famous explorer. I am ten years old and very clever. I speak Latin (just enough to order a cup of tea) and Greek (just enough to send it back) and I have explored lots of the world. I am four feet two inches tall and four feet three inches tall in my hiking boots. I have a large pith helmet and lots of fly-swats. I also have an atlas of the world called Atlas of the World, which I use when I go exploring. Being famous and important means I get invited to important places. Like this place –

(I forgot what the place was called and had to look inside the Bishop's hat. It said "Property of St. Paul's Cathedral." I think I annoyed him.) -

St.Paul's Cathedral.

(Some people clapped here and I think I heard someone say, "Is this the bingo?") Once, not long ago I was asked to explore a lesser part of Egypt called the Valley of the Baby Camels. The place is full of little pyramids and I climbed up the first one easily.

(The bishop interrupted me and, holding onto his hat, said, "Could you get to the point?" and I hissed, "Yes, it wasn't a very high pyramid." Seems he meant could I get to the point of the story. The audience were getting restless and had only come for the bingo.)

And so, from this wooden chest I present the Nail Clippings of Kaki-Tartar. These Clippings I personally found in the Kaki Tomb where they had laid amongst other Egyptian artefacts for thousands of years.

(That got an Ooooo from the audience)

The Nail Clippings of Kaki-Tartar, ladies and gentlemen – the eighth wonder of the world. But the Royal Navigational Society who are "very important" *(I made quotation marks in the air to show I was being SARCASTIC)* said there can only be SEVEN wonders of the world. In this pouch are the last clippings from the last toes of Kaki-Tartar.

(And that was the bit where I supposed to pull out the nail clippings and pass them around, but the pouch was EMPTY. I didn't know where they had gone or what had happened to them. It was SOOOOO embarrassing. The rest of my speech was supposed to be all about the history of Kaki-tart but without the nail clippings I was stumped. I quickly said, "It's bingo time!" winked at the bishop and legged it down the aisle.)

***

And this is where Florence's short speech ends, but it is where the real story begins. The Nail Clippings of Kaki-Tartar carried a dark and foul curse. Only a stupid person would ignore it. Florence, it seems, was very stupid. But did she actually discover them in the first place? Indeed she did. I have the documents to prove it. But at the very moment she wanted to reveal them to the British public they vanished into thin air. A strange occurrence and one that was to get stranger. What became of the Nail Clippings? Perhaps this cutting from the London Times of 21st July 1893 may shed a little light –

Nigel Tattle's Diary of Social Affairs and Events

It seems everyone is talking about Rupert Creamingly, the finest beautician in London. Everyone knows he is the personal make-up artist to Prime Minister Gladstone, but here is something only a very few people know. It seems dear Rupert was at work in his beauty parlour the other day and had just put the finishing touches to Lady Fop's Hair Net. I am told the good Lady shrieked in delight at the result of Rupert's work. She was convinced she was to be the talk of Ascot, but, between you and me, it was the huge spot on the end of her nose which would draw attention. Once more Lady Fop shrieked and dear Rupert ran over, clutching the bill onto which he had just scribbled a few extra noughts, to find out what was troubling her ladyship.
"My beauty spot!" She shrieked again in a voice that could grate cheese. Rupert tried to placate her, "Yes, her ladyship has the finest beauty spot in England!"
"Not anymore., She responded, removing the mirror from her face,. "Someone has squeezed it!"
Of course, this all could be mere gossip, but I am told Lady Fop now attends social functions with a small set of curtains in front of her nose.
This is the first recording of the Nail Clippings wreaking havoc. More was to come. Strange reports could be found on almost every page of every newspaper – tales of blackboards being scraped in empty classrooms, bottoms being pinched at the opera, peas being flicked across the dining room at the Ritz Hotel. I

also uncovered this entry in the Ward Diary of Battersea Childrens Hospital. Nurse Crickle wrote: "Upon taking Master Tompkinson's temperature I momentarily left to allow him to sleep. On my return he sat up straight and smiled at me and said, "Thank you for scratching my foot, nursey." I couldn't bring myself to tell him I hadn't even been in the room."

So it was plain to all and sundry the naughty nail clippings were running amok around London. Who was to know what vile villainy they were to cause? It was a devilish tale bordering on the slightly eerie not far from outlandishly weird.

Our next piece of evidence in this tale takes the form of a letter - a letter written by the hand Edwina Scoop and read by the eyes of Florence Gallop. Edwina was a columnist and reporter on the London Times and had written many times to Florence without receiving a single reply. This letter, it seems, was her last attempt.

Dearest Misstress Gallopp,
I is writtin an artickle for the noospaper and wanted to ask you sum things. My name is Edwina Scoop and these is my quiztions –
a) Cud you comment on the dizzyperance of the Nale Clippings, please?
b) Did you no everyone in London finks you is pullin off a scam and you relly no where they are?
c) If you produce the Nales this Noospaper will gif you £100,000 in money.
Yours fafffuly, Miss Edwina Scoop.

Now what was Florence thinking as she read this ill-spelled and slightly scruffy letter? £100,000 could have come in very useful for an explorer with many parts of the world still to see. £100,000 could be spent on much needed new equipment and travel plans. So what was Florence thinking? This is her reply –

Dearest Miss Scoop,
How delightful to receive such an intelligent and well-thought out letter.
These are my answers to your questions.
a) The rumours of the disappearance of the Nail Clippings are greatly
exaggerated (see answer c).
b) It is not a scam, but I can now reveal the Nail Clippings are safely
hidden away.
c) I am a serious explorer and do not do it for profit. I can show you
the Nail Clippings, but want the money first. I need to buy some new
wellingtons for a forthcoming expedition. And some gloves.
Yours sincerely, Florence Gallop (miss)

Dearest Misstress Gallopp,
I has ad a word wiff my bozz and ee saise that we can giff you the
money but you as to giff us the Nales. If you as em. We will haff a
meetin at the Roil Naffigaichunal Sositty on Fryday at noon o'clock.
Bring the Nales and you shall haff the money.
Fafffuly Edwina Scoop.

What an invitation! What an opportunity! What appalling spell-
ing! How could Florence refuse? But did Florence really know
the whereabouts of the Nail Clippings or was she really pulling
off a scam to earn £100,000? Perhaps the next item may reveal
more. It is the transcript of a police interview with Florence Gallop recorded on to the new wax gramophone on 31st August
1893 about tea-time –

***

Clapham Police Station Official Police Recording of Interview between Miss Florence Gallop and Constable Stubble.

Constable Stubble: Could you tell us a little about your doings on
the night in question.

Florence Gallop: I did a naughty thing.

(Here there is a long, long pause and we hear only the crackle of the record and embarrassed shuffling of the officer.)

Constable Stubble: Could you tell us a little more?

Florence Gallop: Certainly. On the night in question I was sitting on the edge of my bath thinking about my fate.

Constable Stubble: Why were you thinking about your feet?

Florence Gallop: Not feet, fate. If I failed to produce the Nail Clippings I would become a laughing stock of the Royal Navigational Society.

Constable Stubble: And you would lose the £100,000 promised you by the London Times.

Florence Gallop: I do wish you would stop interrupting. I have a lot to say and this is a very short record. I was sitting on the edge of the bath when suddenly I saw my feet.

Constable Stubble: Your fate?

Florence Gallop: No, my feet. And I saw the nails on the end of my toes. I swiftly grasped a pair of nail clippers and set to work.

Constable Stubble: Where did you get the nail clippers, miss?

Florence Gallop: I bought them that very morning from the chemist.

Constable Stubble: And do you have the receipt?

Florence Gallop: No, whatever has that to do with my story?

Constable Stubble: Just checking.

Florence Gallop: Well stop it. I clipped every nail off every toe and by the end I had a small pile of slightly whiffy toenail clippings. Only an experienced eye could prove they did not belong to an Egyptian Mummy. The next day I breakfasted on quails eggs and cheese. I dressed in my Khaki jacket, puttees and pith helmet. I took my fly net from the cupboard and set to work on the second part of my plan.

(At this point a distinct snoring can be heard.)

Florence Gallop: Are you listening, little man?

(It seems Florence bangs the table here and the needle hops from the record. The interview is replaced by the sound of the Clapham Police Choir singing a selection of music hall songs which Stubble clearly thought he was recording over).

***

Sadly, there is no further recording of the police interview, however further evidence was to prove Florence Gallop's undoing. Two days after the events she related to Officer Stubble this appeared in the London Times –

IDIOT SPOTTED CLIMBING BIG BEN
Special Report by Colin Scratch

St. Martins Lane, the busy hub of London's market trading. Not far from where I stand a turnip seller hawks his wares, a mobile barber goes about his business followed by small boy with a dust pan and brush. Behind me signs swing in the breeze declaring their owners' trades –

"Ears Pierced While You Wait!"

"Cast Iron Sinks!"

All was well and proper in this bustling lane yesterday, until a STRANGE OCCURRENCE OCCURRED.

The sight of a small girl was not an unusual one on these streets, but the sight of a small girl dressed in a pith helmet and hiking boots carrying a fly swat was. The girl climbed onto a small soap box she was carrying and tried to attract the crowd's attention. Not something easy to do in the cacophonous surroundings. She then produced a small car horn, honked it loudly and waited for silence.

"My name is Florence Gallop," an eye-witness said she said, "And I am going to re-capture the runaway Nail Clippings!" This drew a loud cheer from the crowd and a fishmonger enthusiastically slapped a fish on his counter.

"Many people think", the eye-witness continued she continued,

45

"I have stolen the Nail Clippings. Well, it's simply not true. Look."
Here she rolled-up both her trouser legs and sleeves. This shocking act caused a gasp of embarrassment and the fishmonger
stopped slapping his fish. It was quickly agreed the girl did not
have the nail clippings and could she cover up her arms and legs?
The girl's plan was clearly well prepared. She grabbed her soapbox and her car horn and cried, "To Big Ben!" and she set off
pursued by the curious street traders and their customers.

Big Ben, the most famous of all London's landmarks, has donged
and dinged the hours for many years, but yesterday it was the
location of a STRANGE EVENT.
Florence Gallop appeared at the base of the noble tower and announced to all her new followers she believed the Nail Clippings
were hidden somewhere on the tower. How she came across this
information is a mystery. And she refused to answer questions.
She placed her flyswat, soapbox and carhorn on the ground,
cracked her knuckles and then did an odd thing. An eye-witness
claimed she patted her pockets as if looking for something. She
patted them again, a little more frantically and then finally peered
up her sleeve and sighed. What was she hiding?

Then her climb began. Up and up she went, higher and higher. The
perilous clamber was keenly watched by the gathered throng. A
raven swooped passed the girl as she neared her half-way point.
And then the girl stopped. This is where some confusion arose —
many folk say she reached into a small crevice on the tower, but
others say she reached up her sleeve. Whichever it was a small
bag appeared and she waved it triumphantly.
"I have found the Nail Clippings of Kaki-Tartar," an eye-witness
said she yelled. Unfortunately, to wave the bag entailed her removing a hand from the tower and that is when she lost her grip
and slipped.

She whooped and cursed as she curled and tumbled through the air, but the story ends happily. It also ends grottily. Florence Gallop was saved from death by landing in something soft and sticky and brown. Unfortunately, the London Times will not allow me to write any more about the sticky substance into which she fell so I shall have to leave it to your imagination.

And if you have no imagination here is something that may help. It is the transcript of a speech given by Mr. Ernest Runns, who was the Star Guest at the Annual Manure Shifters Ball in 1893. He was the Star Guest because of his involvement in the above occurrence. I managed to find a copy of the speech, wiped it down and place it before you. You may have to hold your nose.

"So there I am happily trotting down the street with Flusher pulling me cart and Mrs. Runns jabbering in me ear. I got two hundred weight of top quality poop to get to Peckham before night fall. Now me and the wife have been married longer than either of us has fingers and toes to count so I'd given up listening to her long since. But what I did hear was this. It was a sort of squelchy, sploshy ploppy sound and was coming for me cart. So I gives the reins to the wife and turns around and there before my very eyes is a happarition covered head to toe in poop. I stares at it and it stares back. Then it says, "I am Florence Gallop take me to the Royal Navigational Society." Well, I'm not happy about this. Not happy at all and I says, "What you doing in my muck? You're getting it dirty!" and it says, "I am Florence Gallop take me to the Royal Navigational Society." So I snatched back the reins from the wife who was still jabbering away and I gees up Flusher. It just so happens we was just around the corner from the place what she wants and I drops her off. Seemed a nice girl. I wish she hadn't shook my hand though."

So the question on your spotty tongue is what happened next? For that information we must consult the Official Archivist of the Royal Navigational Society, Mr. Edward Quilt, whom I interviewed for my records. The moment Florence burst into the Grand Hall of the Royal Navigational Society with the bag of toe nails in her hand and her clothes splattered with manure was clearly one he would remember for a very long time.

Grimpen: Could you tell the readers a little ...
Quilt: Friday, about twelve noon it was and the clock had just stopped its donging. Into the Grand Hall of the Royal Navigational Society squelched a short thing and it was ponging like a stable. It had a mean look in its eye and the fellows of the society parted like a herd of startled buffalo. I checked my side arm for protection and my whiskey for ice and watched the spectacle unfold.
"I am Florence Gallop! And I have the Nail Clippings of Kaki-Tartar!" she bellowed. We had already been alerted this may occur and members of the press had gathered in expectation. A gaggle of reporters, clutching their pens and papers, crowded around the stinking child and began questioning her in an abrupt manner. I ordered another whiskey from a passing waiter and tried to eavesdrop.

"The nail clippings currently running amok in London are not the Nail Clippings of Kaki- Tartar! For they are here!"
And with that she drew a pouch from her jacket and from it produced ten toe nails. She shifted the remains of a fulsome lunch and laid them out on the Grand Banqueting Table. There was a gasp of admiration. Sir Albert Toot, our esteemed chairman, cleared his throat and was about to make a speech of gratitude when another voice piped up from the back, "Stop!" it said. Its owner was amongst the crowd of reporters, "I am Edwina Scoop of the London Times and those are not the Nail Clippings of

Kaki-Tartar."

"Yes, they are! And I claim my £100,000."

"No, they're not!"

Two ladies head to head in a set-to like this can be a horrible and sickening sight so I found a nearby chair and made myself comfy.

"And I can prove it!"

Now all the members of the society muttered and looked about. Sir Albert Toot gestured for the Edwina Scoop to step forward. And she did.

"In my hand I have a receipt!" She pulled a tattered slip of paper from her pocket and held it aloft. She continued, "A receipt for a set of nail clippers!"

Another gasp ran through the room followed by a confused snort and then an awkward pause. The pause was Edwina's and she was using it for dramatic effect. She glanced at the reporters and you could hear a pen drop in the silence. Edwina Scoop stomped up to the stench-riddled Gallop and held the receipt before her mudded face.

"Read what it says!" she ordered.

Gallop flicked something from her eye and gazed at the receipt. She muttered something.

"Speak up!" Scoop ordered again.

"It says, 'Receipt for One Set of Nail Clippers Purchased by Florence Gallop!'."

Suddenly hundreds of pencils began scribbling on hundreds of note pads and someone far at the back began wittering into one of those new telephone gadgets.

"Now you may be wondering how I came by this receipt?"

The fellows of the society nodded as loudly as they could over the sound of the scribbling pencils.

"I had been corresponding with Florence Gallop in the hope of gaining an interview for my paper. I had adopted the writing style of a simpleton in the hope she may take sympathy on me. She did, but the reply contained more than just answers to my question. Florence Gallop had accidentally folded this receipt into her letter!"

From the corner of my eye I noticed Constable Stubble of Scotland Yard come into view. He strode stealthily over to the hubhub and began to observe the goings-on.
"Constable - arrest this woman!"
Constable Stubble looked about a little nervously and said, "I can't do that, Miss Scoop." Edwina was clearly not a woman to be tangled with and Stubble was about to get tangled. "Why not?"
The constable lowered his voice and said, "We ain't got no evidence!"
Scoop gestured towards the whiffy nail clippings spread out on the table.
"This is the evidence!"
Stubble adjusted his tie, polished his whistle and finally wiped his helmet.
"But we don't know they are hers!" he said nodding towards Florence Gallop.
"Ha!" yelped Florence pointing a manure-covered finger at Edwina.
"Remove her shoes and socks!" replied Scoop, softly.

Within seconds Florence was laying on her back on the Grand Banqueting Table in the Grand Hall of the Royal Navigational Society with her socks being tugged from her little feet by eager journalists, a reluctant policeman and a giggling bishop.
Ten tiny toes wiggled by the soup bowl. At the other end of her body Florence Gallop's face was frozen in an expression of impending doom. Scoop took the first toenail and held it in the air for all to see. She inspected it closely, nodded sagely then tried it

against Gallop's left big toe. Every pair of eyes in the room stared intently as she did so. It fitted perfectly. One by one each and every toenail on the table was tried against a toe and one by one every toenail fitted every toe.

As Constable Stubble stepped forward with his handcuffs a camera flash went off and the case was proven beyond doubt.

Now most readers would think that was the end of this particularly grotty tale. But there is just a little more. I have in my collection a photographic plate. It is the photograph of a wall - the wall of the cell in which Florence Gallop was imprisoned. And upon this wall is scrawled some words in the handwriting of Florence Gallop. I have studied the photograph under a magnifying glass and this is what I believe is written:

"The moon gazes through the cell window and all I hear is tap-tap, tap-tap, tap-tap on the cell door, night after night. Then tonight through the barred windows tip-tapped brown and aged toenails. They are tapping at my water bowl as a write this. They tap-tap-tap closer and closer and closer. Tap-tap-tap..."

The Septic Tale of Dr.Jekyll and Mr.Sheen

Clean your ears out before embarking on this story. It will help you hear better. It will also get rid of the horrible mushrooms growing there.

CRASH!!!!

That was the eye-wateringly, knee-bangingly, nose-wipingly terrifying sound which announced the beginning of this sad and sorrowful story. It was the sound of a fine stained glass window, which was once the pride of the Boddlington family, smashing and crashing into quadrillions of tiny sharp shards. And the smash happened in the middle of the night! Oooooooooooooooooooooh!

The Boddlingtons had lived at No.1, Snottly Street (not far from a very nice new post box) since the Bore War of 1850 - which is about ten to seven. The stained glass window was the most famous part of the entire house and now there was a large hole in it about the size of a well-fed rhino or skinny elephant depending how you look at these things. Upon hearing the shattering, Lord "Envelope" Boddlington ambled forth from his bed chamber to see what had caused the naughty noise. As he yawned, sniffled, hiccuped and scratched parts of his body we won't mention, he gazed, bleary-eyed through the hole at the towering, filth-pumping chimney at the bottom of Snottly Street.
"What a big hole!" he muttered, "About the size of fifty gerbils."
Lord Boddlington had a strange way of measuring things. He half expected to find an interloper, perhaps a rogue, perhaps some manner of vagabond. Instead he saw something very surprising. So surprising, in fact, his wig nearly leaped off his head and hid behind the curtains.

"Slap me with a jelly fish!" he exclaimed, adjusting his wig. But, as it was his butler's day off, no one carried out his order.

He surveyed his drawing room.

He sniffed, he snuffed, he puffed. He didn't know what to say.

All his furniture had been rearranged!

And not only that, but the glass had been swept up!

And not only that, but every nook and cranny was spick and span. His entire house had been cleaned from roof to cellar!

"This is the work of...the work of...the most dastardly villain in all of London!" he announced to no one in particular, "This is the work of the Phantom Good-Deed-Doer!"

And had there been a pipe organ in the room at the time it would have played a mysterious and dramatic chord, but there wasn't so it didn't. Lord Boddlington gazed through the hole in his window at the chimney and sighed, sniffed again, hugged his teddy bear and went back to bed.

The home of much-respected and well-loved doctor, Timothy Jekyll, was not far from No.1 Snottly Street and in it was his servant, Sam Sweller, cleaning and polishing the rooms and awaiting the return of his master. The hall clock struck seventeen times which, as the clock had been broken for years, told Sam the time was nine o'clock. At that precise moment the dishevelled and confused doctor burst into the room. His coat was torn, his hat was bent and there was a faint whiff of cleaning fluids about his person. What was Sam to make of all this? Where had his master been till this hour?

Sam pondered and wondered as he dusted the cat.

"What am I to make of all this? Where has my master been till this hour? Why does he smell of cleaning fluids? What has become of my mop? And why am I dusting the cat?"

Sam said nothing but watched carefully as Doctor Jekyll stumbled into his office, slammed and locked the door then squidged a bit of putty in the keyhole because he knew Sam liked looking through it.

"Ha!" snarled Jekyll.
"Ha!" snarled Edgar the doctor's faithful black raven, perched on a tottering pile of medical books.
"That should keep that pokey-nosed servant's eaves-dropping ears out of my business!" And he stuck out his tongue at the door.
"Ha!" snarled Edgar once more. Only Edgar knew the doctor's secret and it was a shocking, knee-knocking secret of vile villainy. Would you like to hear it? Please say, "Yes" at the book. Thank you. You see, Jekyll had been experimenting with the human mind. He had been dabbling with the inner workings of the human psyche - the good and the evil. And he had been trying to separate the two. So far he has only managed to isolate one… and not the one he was expecting.

As dawn broke the next day and the sun shone out over a thriving London, Sam Sweller found himself dusting around the laboratory.
"What a to-do last night, eh, Edgar?"
"Ha!" said the raven.
"I wonder what that doctor of ours is really up to?"
Edgar looked from side to side then jumped from the tottering pile of books over to the desk. Sam watched, bewildered as the raven started banging his little black beak on a pile of papers.
"What's that, Edgar? You want me to read these papers?"
Edgar banged his beak more furiously on the pile.
"But these are Doctor Jekyll's professional notes. I can't read those."
Edgar banged his little beak even more.
"Oh, very well, Edgar, as you insist, but just a sneaky peak."

Sam carefully placed down his duster and slid a piece of parchment from under Edgar, then held it to the light and read it, "Gentlemen, do you suffer from excessive armpit hair? Then visit the best armpit barber in all of London..."

Edgar screeched, snatched the paper from Sam and handed him another.

"The Top Secret Diary of Doctor Timothy Jekyll..."

And Sam started to read.

"Extra! Extra! Read all about it!"

The paper boy stood on the corner of the hustling, bustling street shouting out the latest blood-curdling headlines, "London Times cries out for justice!"

From out of the dank shadows of a nearby alley slunk Doctor Jekyll. He stood and watched the paper boy.

"The Phantom Good-Deed-Doer had struck again! Baroness Dribbling-Teabag has her entire mansion redecorated whilst on holiday!"

Doctor Jekyll stepped towards the boy, menacingly.

"Give me a paper!" he snarled.

"That'll be a penny, please, sir," said the boy, handing over a copy.

"I have no money!"

"Then I'll have it back then," said the boy, grasping for the paper.

"Stay away!" snarled the doctor who seemed to be doing an awful lot of snarling, "Otherwise..." and then he produced a beautifully laundered and ironed handkerchief, "I will wipe your nose!"

The boy screamed, "Extra! Extra! Read all about it! Paper boy threatened with handkerchief in broad daylight! Bravely stands his ground for seconds then runs off home to his mummy!"

And so, screaming the boy ran off and Doctor Jekyll started to read of his alter ego's adventures of the previous night.

The next morning the door of the doctor's home banged open

and its owner once more returned in a shattered and tattered state. He was bemused and confused and splashed with pink emulsion paint. Sam, his ever useful servant, was usefully sitting in the laboratory cupboard pretending to dust a few paperclips. The door was slightly open and Sam, unseen by the prying eyes of his master, overheard every word to come out of his sad mouth. "This is the end, Edgar! The end, I say! No more cleaning and dusting and swilling and mopping! No more do-gooding for me! I intend putting a stop to it all this very day!

And with those final words he snapped Sam's mop in two pieces. "Eeek!" the 'eeek' you just heard came from the mouth of Sam and his mouth, like Sam, was in the cupboard.

Doctor Jekyll ripped open the door and stared down at his trembling servant.

"You!" snarled the doctor. I wonder when he will stop snarling?

"Me!" said Sam, pointing to himself so they both knew who they were talking about, "I know everything! I have read the diary! I have seen your secret stash of polish and sprays!" Sam drew himself up to his full height which was not very high and said, "And you broke my mop!"

The doctor was incensed. He snarled (again) and growled and hissed.

Sam, keeping his employer at a distance with one end of the mop, said, "I shall tell the London Times everything!"

But it was all no use, the doctor, by far the stronger of the two, overpowered his little odd job man. He slipped a tin of "Spruce It Up" polish from his waistcoat pocket and held it under Sam's nose. The room started to wobble and sway and swing and turn inside out, upside down and back to front. The doctor caught Sam as he fell into a deep, deep sleep. The doctor cackled and snorted and, when he couldn't think of anything else to do, he snarled.

When Sam awoke he found himself in a copper bath wearing only his pants. The room was lit by a spluttering candle and the muttering doctor stood nearby brandishing hot water and soap. "It is time for my Final Clean!" he said, stalking back and forth, waving the soap threateningly. "I am one of the finest scientists in all of London. I have split the human mind in two. I thought I may have isolated the evil side, but no, oh, no. I ended up isolating the nice, goodie-goodie part. For the last week my alterego, Mr.Sheen, has been breaking into people's homes across London and... " he could barely bring himself to say the last words, "... cleaning them!"

He peered down at the trembling Sam and spat out his final words.

"If you mutter so much as a single, solitary syllable of what you've seen you will given the biggest, best scrubbing of your life!" He pointed the sponge at Sam and the sunlight glinted off his manic eye. Sam whimpered slightly, placed a finger on his lips then placed another finger on that finger. That shows serious it was.

Having secured his odd odd job man, the doctor began concocting a final, huge double dose of do-good-juice. This was the vile vial he'd been quaffing from over the past few days. A noxious concoction full of the most stomach-knottingly, ear-wipingly, goose-bumpingly gross stuff you could ever imagine. Go on imagine it now! Nope, it's far worse than that. Edgar hopped back and forth and tried to dissuade his master from imbibing another tot, but his attempts were fruitless. He hopped back on the tottering pile of medical books and watched amazed as his master took a final giddy gulp and slowly, very slowly started to transform.

First his ears popped,

then his nose straighten with a crack,

then his hair grew long and luxurious,

then his eyes shimmered until they turned perfect blue,

then his back snapped straight, his chin became shaven, his nose unhairy and he turned to his goggle-eyed raven and said, "Call me, Mr.Sheen!"

Rubber gloves appeared and every possible cleaning implement you could imagine pop-pop-pooped into his hands.

A bright twinkle danced on his teeth and with a manic cackle he left the house.

Constable Stubble of Marlborough Police Station was renowned throughout all of Great London as being one of the most eagle-eyed coppers ever to blow his whistle on the streets. So it was no surprise then, when Sam entered the police station wearing only his underpants, Constable Stubble said, "You are wearing only your underpants!" That's why Constable Stubble earned 52 shillings a week and got to take his uniform home at weekends!

In a hurried speech, full of stumbles and bumbles, which I won't bother writing out in full as you already know what has happened and I'm getting tired, Sam recounted the horrid events of the last few days. Everything about the diary, the mop and especially why he was only wearing underpants. Constable Stubble waved his truncheon in the air and blew his whistle three times he was so excited.

"We must set forth after this vile villain and bring him to justice and to the police station!"

Pausing only to wrap Sam in an old sack which he kept for storing his handcuffs in, Constable Stubble set off on the trail of the Phantom Good-Deed-Doer!

The large chimney at the end of Snottley Street had been pumping out foggy smog and smoggy fog since before anyone could remember and a lot of folks in Snottley Street could remember a lot of things. Year upon year it had spat its sickly stench into the streets of old London City - and each plume of smoke had weaved and snaked its way into the mouths and noses and ears and other parts of everyone in London. Before long Constable Stubble in his uniform, Sam in his sack, and Edgar in his feathers had tracked down the trail of Mr.Sheen. A slimey line of cleaning fluid had dripped and dribbled and led them to the exact bottom of the belching chimney. They looked up. Tottering on the tip-top was Mr.,Sheen! He stood there looking down defiantly and waving his duster threateningly.

"So I bid farewell to this wretched world!" he bellowed. "No more will I slink through the underworld mopping and dusting and polishing and buffing. This is my final tidy!"

And with that cry of victory he leaped, jumped, hopped and plummeted into the foggy murk of the chimney. Swallowed by the filthy fog! Constable Stubble, and the crowd which had gathered around, fell as silent as a mushroom. And then a deathly scream was heard. Edgar swooped upwards and into the gaping hole and shortly returned holding only a duster.
"Do something, constable!" shouted Sam.
"I can't, sir, I'm afraid he got clean away..."
And the Phantom Good-Deed-Doer was never seen or heard of ever again.

Many months later, at the reading of Doctor Jekyll's will, Sam was a little surprised to find all the contents and deeds to the house had been left to... Edgar the Raven! Luckily, Edgar kept Sam on as his servant to clean out his bird cage.

BEE

Look what's happened to me
I've just been stung by a bee
It seems an awful lot of money
£20 for a jar of honey.

KEEP YOUR DISTANCE

"Keep Your Distance"
says the sign
on the motorway.

But I do keep my distance.
I keep it in a box.
It's a very long box.

iT...

Hide in your rough book,
Don't let teacher see it
Put it in your pencil case
Don't let teacher see it.

Slip it in your lunch box,
Don't let teacher see it
Put it in your pocket
But don't let teacher see it.

Lose it in your PE kit
Hide it! Be a mate,
Don't let teacher see it.
Oh, oh! Oh, no! Too late!

SCENTED

My little brother, on Valentine's Day
Came rushing down the hall.
Then I heard him, panting, say
"For you a card, pink, quite small."

"Everywhere I wented
I ranned as fast as I canned!"
I said "A valentine's card? Was it scented?"
He said, "No, delivered by hand!"

PROFESSIONAL WRITER

I'm a professional writer
Today I wrote the word "Mother"
I've refilled my pencil
And sharpened my pen –
So tomorrow I may write another.

CASTLE CLANG
The Reading of the Cheese.

Aunt Dollop hopped gleefully from foot to foot and back again - she only had the usual amount feet so made the most of them. Before she had started hopping gleefully she had leaped from her bed gleefully and before she had leaped from her bed gleefully she been snoring gleefully and it was the most gleeful snore you could possibly imagine. Go on, imagine it! And she had hopped, leaped and snored with glee because today was the day, you see.

Aunt Dollop was of average height, her head reached the top and her legs reached the ground and you couldn't ask for much more in a pair of legs (unless you asked them to hop and leap gleefully because you knew today is the day..) Aunt Dollop's face was a craggy mass of lines and crevices. It was one of those faces that seemed to be a little slower than the brain behind it. So whenever Dollop exclaimed a shriek of delight, which she often did - especially on a Tuesday around bath time - her eyebrows, which on most folks faces would ascend at the same moment as the shriek, would, on Dollops countenance, sit quietly, seemingly twiddling its hairs, until one eyebrow would seem to turn to the other eyebrow and say, "What was that?", "Was that a shriek?" and after a little tonsorial debate they would agree they should leap up in alarm and they would. It was one of those kind of faces. Aunt Dollop heard a distance bird chirrup and ceased hopping. She then rotated three times, faked a burp, tugged her hair and giggled.

This was her daily ritual. It was a royal ritual passed down from father to son to father to son to milkmaid's daughter for generations and generations. And Aunt Dollop, being a stickler for all things ritualistic, stuck to the rules, never varying, never changing. She put on her Tuesday crown, just as she had done every Tuesday for the last 57 years of her royal life and stepped from her bedroom.

Queen Martha was not as excited by the day as her mother. It was almost ten years since her father, King Colin - or "my buried-in-the-garden-husband" as Aunt Dollop called him - had died. Died not on the field of battle, heroically galloping, lance in hand to rescue a damsel in distress - no, King Colin has been attacked by a chicken whilst taking a bath - the king not the chicken - and had been pecked to death. It had been hushed up. She missed him. She had been Queen Martha since she was little and knew nothing other than wearing robes and telling people what to do - which, she had to admit to herself, she quite enjoyed. But she didn't enjoy it half as much as combing her long, golden hair and choosing the finest fabrics to make up the nicest clothes in the country. Oh, and the shouting at people. She liked the shouting, in fact, she was about to do a shout right now.
"Scratch and Sniff!" she bellowed, it was more of scream really.

Scratch and Sniff had been sleeping restlessly in the corridor and leaped to all four feet of their combined legs upon hearing the bellow/scream of their mistress. Scratch and Sniff were the perfect duo, they'd lived the same life, breathed the same air, drunk the same water and shared the same nits their entire lives. This particularly morning they helped each other stand up, tussled and swiftly combed each other's hair, dusted each other down and allowed each other a large, loud, grotty yawn before each in unison knocking on Queen Martha's door and stepping into her huge bedroom.

"I didn't say enter, doofuses!" bellowed (or screamed) Martha, wiggling her hair brush in a threatening manner.
Scratch said, "We thought it was an emergency, your diddleship."
Martha considered his answer. Emergency? Diddleship? Scratch and Sniff were wont to invent words and phrases willy-nilly like "willy" and "nilly" when they were stuck for the correct protocol. And Scratch had decided that upon discovering a royal personage in bed brandishing a hairbrush then said majesty must be referred to as her diddleship. She liked diddleship.

"Good answer, but I have a better question!"
Scratch grabbed Sniff by the scruff of his scruffy neck and bowed him, Sniff stood up and did the same to Scratch. This is how they traditionally bowed.
"And this is my question..."
Scratch and Sniff were about to bow each other again, but Queen Martha wiggled her hairbrush again.
"Is it the day?"
Scratch and Sniff exchanged a look, a shrug and grabbed each other's little beards and tugged on each. Both heads nodded. Today was, indeed, the day.
"You've got to get it right. You've got to get it right!" said a quiver-

ing voice. The voice belonged to the mouth that belonged to the face of trainee wizard, Gleek. He often spoke to himself and often answered himself, too. He often had huge arguments with himself and sometimes made himself sit in the naughty wizard corner. He spoke to himself because the rest of the folk in Castle Clang rarely listened to him and those who did usually said, "Who said that?" It had been traditional to have a wizard in your castle for more years than anyone could count, if anyone could count. And Gleek was the Wizard of Castle Clang. At this moment, at the earliest point of the day, Gleek was hurriedly putting the final finishing touches to his invention. He stood back from the table and admired it.

"Well done!" he said, "Thank you!" he answered.

Gleek was not too thin and not too fat. He was not too old and not young - in fact, he was just right and just right now he was very proud.

"That will do the job!" He placed his tools on the table and gave himself a little clap. A smile wiggled on his lips and he suppressed a giggle.

Before his wizardy eyes, sitting quietly on the table, newly brought into existence - the invention not the table - was Gleek's New Invention. A Dragon Detector. He ran his eyes over the fine new creation. To my eyes and most probably to your eyes it would look like a bucket, because, basically, it was a bucket.

"But it's not just a bucket!" explained Gleek, having imagined someone saying to him, "That's just a bucket!"

And he began to explain - partly he was also rehearsing his speech to her diddleship whom later in the day (the day) would point her hair brush at it and say, "That's just a bucket!"

"No, no, your most marvellous majesticals! This (and here I will leave a dramatic pause, twiddle my sleeves and wink) this is a

Dragon Detector! Where upon which her majesty will throw her hair brush in the air with glee, perhaps indulge in a couple of happy hops and say, "Gleek, you are the finest of all wizards, I have ignored you for too long - please feel free to help yourself the contents of my treasure chest!"

He gave himself another clap - imagined receiving an award for wizardy - then decided it was time he put his clothes on.

Breakfast in Castle Clang was an event once described by one of their few visitors as "Arggghhh, that stings! I want my teddy. My head hurts!"

Scratch was buttering the cornflakes and Dog the dog was licking clean the breakfast plates. A big bowl of salt sat in the centre of the grand banqueting table and Sniff was just adding a little sugar to taste when a cough came to the door. Sniff had never heard a door cough before though once he thought he heard a catflap sneeze. He shrugged loudly as Scratch who made a "Don't-be-stupid-and-open-the-door" gesture at him, which is not an easy gesture to do. Try it, we'll wait. But Queen Martha wouldn't wait because she was the one at the door and the one doing the coughing.

"Fanfare!" she hissed under her breath and over her teeth.

Scratch and sniff immediately ceased what they were doing and picked up two teapots which they held to each others lips and blew. The sound was not quite a fanfare and not quite music, but as they couldn't afford real musicians it was the best they could so they did it.

Queen Martha, waving in a majestical majesterial manner, placed one of her two feet in the hall no sooner had she done this than from her left appeared Aunt Dollop screeching, "It's the day!" and from her right appeared Gleek shouting, "It's not a bucket! It's not a bucket!"

All three became wedged in the door - this was far from regal. Scratch and Sniff placed the teapot on the table and wondered what to do. Aunt Dollop, a sticky stickler for ritual, wondered what was the correct royal way to deal with the situation and Gleek just wondered.

Queen Martha sighed the sigh she had sighed many days during her reign and said, "I think tugging may be in order!"
Scratch gave Sniff a confused and quizzical glance who, not sure what to do with it, passed it onto Queen Martha.
"Tugging!" she bellowed, partly because she wanted unwedging and partly because she'd spotted some tasty looking bacon yoghurt.

Scratch and Sniff looked each other up and down and then down and up and then held hands. They started pulling each other back and forth (and after that forth and back.)
"Not you!" squawked the queen, "Us!"
Scratch and Sniff bowed each other and scurried over to the doorway.
They tugged and pulled at whichever limb stuck out and after a few moments of un-ladylike, un-regal, un-believable behaviour all three were pulled through the door with an almost audible pop. Pop!

Queen Martha adjusted her crown, which had fallen over her eyes, Gleek clutched and checked his bucket ("It's not a bucket!" he whispered to himself) and Aunt Dollop had her face in the salt and sugar. "Hmmmm!"
The odd group slurped and burped their way through a bizarre

breakfast. The buttered cornflakes soon disappeared leaving a small pile of corny crumbs for Dog the dog to nibble. The potato sausages were a huge success and everyone guzzled the soil tea eagerly. It wasn't long before everyone had forgotten the wedged-in-the-door-situation and were soon chatting and chittering away like they'd known each other for years, which they had done, but they just occasionally forgot it.

Gleek held a piece of toast in the air, "A toast!" he announced.
Aunt Dollop held up a sausage, "A sausage!"
Gleek stood up, adjusted his tunic, scratched his bald head, pondered, wondered and wandered around the table. All eyes followed him between burps and slurps and finally he held his finger in the air.
"Ah!" he proudly announced.
"Ah!" said everyone else, though their "ah" was more of a "get-on-with-it-the-chocolate-porridge-is-starting-to-go-cold" kind of "ah"
"Ah!" said Gleek, pacing the table. Not next to the table, but on it.
"Ah!" they repeated but this "Ah!" was more of a "don't-hurt-yourself-on-a-slippy-kipper" "Ah!"
"I have an announcement to announce!" he swirled the toast in the air and dramatically bellowed, "Dearest folk of Castle Clang, many days have passed since the demise of our Great King Colin, may he rest in pieces, pecked to death, as we sadly know, by the chicken from hell. Since that time his finest daughter Martha has assumed his role - but what, you may be wondering, does her future and the future of all us Clangites have in store?"
He stabbed the air with his finger and the porridge with his foot. "Tonight is the night!"
Everyone clapped loudly. Scratch and Sniff clapped each other's hands. "Because today is the day!"

Aunt Dollop was thrilled royal protocol was being observed so well. Queen Martha was delighted because it was all about her. Gleek was thrilled because everyone was looking at him. Scratch and Sniff were pleased no one had spotted what was floating in the tea and only Dog the dog was confused by the yapping of these humans so he occupied himself by licking the wizard's shoe. "Yes, today is the day!!" Gleek threw his arms in the air in a mighty gesture of triumphant at the same time tried to get Dog the dog off his foot. "Today is the day!" He cleared his throat, stepped out of his shoe (which Dog continued licking), did his mighty gesture again which wasn't looking quite so mighty coming from a man with only one shoe and announced,
"Today is the day of the Reading of the Cheese!"

A silence quietly filled the room as silences do and stayed for a while whilst the others exchanged glances. Martha passed a smirk to Dollop who changed it into a grin which she passed to Gleek who tweaked it into a beam and threw towards Scratch and Sniff who, unused to being smirked, grinned or beamed at, made it into a confused sneer.
But the silence soon hitched up its skirts and left the room as Gleek chased it out with the loud words,:
"But first a commercial!"
He continued his wondering wander around the table, but this time in more of a hippity- hoppity kind of way. He was talking about his own subject so was on safe ground, but the table he was on seemed less than safe.
"Now as royal royalty, known and praised throughout our land from here to -" he pointed his pointiest finger out of the window - "there! What is the one thing of which all kings, queens, princes and princesses are most frightened?"
He folded his arms and stared down at faces looking up at him like fish at feeding time. He tapped his foot as he waited, but, as

he had just put his foot back in the chocolate porridge, it was more of a squelch.

Aunt Dollop put her hand in the air. Gleek pointed his second most pointiest finger at her. "Yes?"
"Is is dragons?"
"It is indeed...!"
And at the moment the banquet table, covered with sumptuous food but standing on dodgy legs, collapsed taking Gleek, Dog and the varied selection of scrummy vittles with it.

A few minutes later, Dog was licking clean Gleek's confused and befuddled face. Scratch and Sniff were arguing over which shoe goes on which of the wizard's feet and Dollop was wondering where to dip her eggy soldier. Only Queen Martha held her composure (and her hair brush) and attempted to rise above it all by being extremely Queeny.
"I once had a cat called Mulch!" she said to no one particular and no one in particular was listening.

Gleek leaped to his feet, changed his shoes round and started again.
"So what does a royal family need to warn it if the naughtiest of naughty dragons is looming forth towards their safe and snugly castle?"
No one answered. This was a toughie.
"Right, I'll try again. What do we need to announce the arrival of a snarly, vicious dragon, its tail swinging back and forth alarming sheep and skittling trees? Hmm? Anyone?"
Dollop enjoyed games and thought she was participating in one.
"Is the answer a pointy stick?"
"No, it is not a pointy stick!" sighed Gleek, looking heavenwards and wondering, of all the royal families in the land, why he'd ended

up with this lot.

"Is it something orange with a hinge bit?" shouted Scratch, getting into the spirit.

"Something that mumbles?" countered Sniff.

"A well-trained vole!" giggled Dollop, starting to score points with an eggy finger on her napkin.

"No, no, no, no. None of the above!"

Queen Martha held her brush in the air and the room fell silent. She paused, combed her long golden hair, and slowly said, "A Dragon Detector?"

"Hurrah for the Queen - it is, indeed, a dragon detector. Have a sausage!"

The small, but bewildered, crowd clapped loudly and admiringly. Scratch was about to pat the royal head, but the Queen stopped him with a glare and a dangerous looking sausage.

"So where is this Dragon Detector?"

And with a flourish he had been practising all night, Gleek produced his Dragon Detector. He placed it before the anxious eyes of the group. All four mouths breathed in and all four mouths were about to say something when Gleek shouted, "And it's not a bucket!"

The Dragon Detector was a large (I have to say bucket-like) bowl around the base of which were five ornate and attractive, wooden frogs looking up to the top of the bucket/urn/bowl with their little froggy mouths open.

It was then Gleek, rolled up his wizardly sleeves and decided now was the moment to launch into his explanation.

"I admit, it is somewhat bucketty, but look. Here we fill it to the brim with water and when a dragon comes clumping across fields, snarling and roaring, flames leaping from its hideous mouth, the resulting tremors of each footfall will agitate the bucket and then slopping will begin..."

"Slopping?" inquired Martha.

"The ground will be rumbling and wobbling slightly. The water will slop and casacade into the mouths of the waiting frogs whereupon which each will give off a tiny, mechanical gribbit of my own invention."

He patted the side of the detector/bucket some water slopped and a frog gribbetted.

"Well done, Gleek, what can I say?" said the Queen, "It's very..."

"Thank you, your majesty!" Gleek bowed so low the top of his wizard's hat tickled the Dog. "In fact, it's very, very!"

"Thank you, again, your majesty!" Gleek bowed again.

"Can we read the cheese now?"

Today was cheese reading day.

The dungeon of Castle Clang drip, drip dripped with moist plops of runniness from that leak in the moat they had always intended to mend. Cobwebbed corners cowered in the darkness and the only, only light came from a spluttering candle placed on a rickety table in the centre of the room by the solemn hand of Gleek the Wizard. This was a ritual passed down the years and was treated with utmost of respect by all and sundry especially by Aunt Dollop who loved nothing more than a good ritual and had put red ribbons in her hair especially. The gathered faces of the Clang Royal Family peered out of the darkness like white masks waiting, waiting, waiting. Gleek had placed his Dragon Detector in the corner, out of harm's way.

Suddenly in the gaping silence a knock came to the door.

"Who goes there?" asked the question which had been asked many times down the centuries.

Two muffled voices came from behind the door.

"The cheese!" they almost chanted.

"Whose cheese?" recited Gleek.

"The Queen's Cheese!" the voices responded in unison.

"Come forth the Queen's Cheese!" announced Gleek, with one of his finest wizardry flourishes.

And then slower than the slowest thing you could imagine and then a little slower still the door opened. There, framed in the wooden doorway, were Scratch and Sniff and on a plate on a tray on their hands was a large, innocent looking cheese - with some little holes in it.

Scratch and Sniff entered the room trying to walk in step which proved too difficult and looked more like a rumba.

With great ceremony and just a little pomp they placed the cheese upon the table and stood back. Gleek did another little flourish, cracked his knuckles and said, "The Queen's Cheese!"

"My cheese!" repeated Martha.

"We heard, dear!" said Aunt Dollop.

"And so we begin the Ceremony of the Reading of the Cheese. Passed down the lineage for years beyond our remembrance..."

"He is very good at this, isn't he?" pointed out Aunt Dollop, fingering a ribbon. "Shh!" pointed out Martha.

"In keeping with the oldest tradition we all must now welcome the cheese... your majesty...?"

Martha cleared her throat and said proudly. "Welcome Cheese!"

"Aunt Dollop?"

"Welcome Cheese!"

Scratch and Sniff were not part of the royal family (as far as anyone knew) so were not invited to welcome the cheese but they did both offer a little wave while no one was looking.

"And so I must place myself in a trance..."

Gleek suddenly produced his wand. Not his everyday-turning-people-into-newts-wand - oh, no this was his very-special-use-once-in-a-while-wand - and today was the once in a while day in which he was to use it.

He pointed the wand towards his face. His eyes crossed and focussed on the tip and he spoke in a solemn wizardly way.
"You are feeling woozey, droopy, sleepy..."
Snoring came from the direction of Scratch and Sniff. Soon Gleek, too, was entranced and smiling like he'd just won the prize pig at the village fair.
Gleek started to hum very quietly.
"Why is he humming?" asked Martha.
"Perhaps he doesn't know all the words..." suggested Aunt Dollop.
Suddenly, the wizard's eyelids snapped open and revealed stark staring eyes which were dizzily gazing in the darkness unfocussed and, well, a bit weird.
"I shall read the Cheese!"
And so saying and saying so he slowly (not as slow as the door) placed his wizardy hands on the yellow (and slightly green) cheese. He swayed back and forth and hummed again.
"I think I know this one..." whispered Aunt Dollop, but the end of her sentence was elbowed into silence by Martha who then said, "Speak oh, wise wizard! Predict the future of our lives through the medium of cheese!"

The wizard's pokey little fingers started to scuttle madly over the surface of the mouldy cheese. His eyes were now slammed shut and only the touch of his fingertips could tell him what he found. And what did he find? Everyone looked on enchanted with each mouth drooping opener than the next. His fingertips skedaddled over the cheese stopping here and there to poke a hole or two. He rubbed the cheese and hummed quietly and then once more the scurrying tips began their cheesy investigation. He slid his fingers into one gaping hole, paused, shivered, gagged slightly and moved swiftly onto the next hole. At this hole he giggled like a naughty stoat. He poked the hole again and giggled again. He did this a number of times, before thinking he really ought to get on. So the Reading of the Cheese went on (and on) and on. Scratch and Sniff were both wondering whether to boil another bowl of tea, when Gleek whipped his finger from the final hole, licked it, pointed it in the air and announced, "The Reading the Cheese is complete!"

Aunt Dollop and Queen Martha edged their chairs closer to the table and peered eagerly at their wizard.
"So?" asked the Queen.
The wizard coughed, pondered and then spoke, "The cheese has been touched and the cheese has given forth its prophesy!" He coughed again and pondered again. He rarely received the complete attention of the royal family and was going to make the most of it. "I have run my fingers across its surface and each pokey hole has been investigated. I have learned all that can be learned from a cheese..."
The Queen sighed, "Do get on with it!" she said, "What does the future hold?"
The wizard coughed once more and announced, "All is well! The future is bright, the future holds no dilemmas, worries or concerns. Your majesty will live a fine and full life full of joy and japes. No danger will encroach upon the royal world. No threat or jeopardy will breech the drawbridge of your reign or your castle, come to that. All is, as I say, well!"
"Well!" grinned Dollop.
"Well!" smiled Martha.

Scratch in the furthest corner of the dungeon was holding Sniff's hand in the air and trying to attract the royal attention. Scratch waved the hand vigorously because they had both spotted something. And it was something that might be a problem.

"This deserves a celeberation," said the Queen, "Shall we have more tea?" She turned to Scratch and Sniff and the regal eye landed on the eager hand, flopping back and forth.
"Yes, Scratch?" said the Queen.
"That's Sniff, your majesty, I'm Scratch. You can tell the difference cos I have a mole on the end of my..."
"Get on with it..."
Scratch nudged Sniff to get on with it and he got on with it.
"The frogs are gribbiting!" His eyes gestured into a dark corner of the dark dungeon.

For the fleetingest of moments Queen Martha wondered whether her servant had finally flipped and whether she could return him to the orphanage and ask for a refund.
But Gleek knew what he meant and so did Aunt Dollop and both gulped a dry gulp and quivered slightly.
"What frogs?" asked the Queen, testily.
Scratch and Sniff spoke together - "The frogs on the Dragon Detector!"
(to be continued...)

PIE RECIPE

Take some pastry, three months old,
Check it's rotton and covered with mold.
Cover the base of a baking tin
And then put the following ingredients in –
Some sweepings from a barber's shop,
anything you might find in a mop.
Some cold custard, a used tissue,
Yellow snow and some rabbit poo.
A large portion of old dandruff
A pinch of ear wax and belly button fluff.
Stir in a teaspoon of bathroom waste –
Old cottonbuds and used toothpaste
Half a teaspoon of light grey dust
And then add on top the cardboard crust.
Garnish with a handful of snot
And bake for three days til it's nice and hot.
Top it off with a long dead worm
And serve to your teacher
on the last day of term.

I'M A POET

Gurgle, furgle, wurgle, flob,
Urgle, turgle, mugle, zob.
Flishy, flushy, mushy, tob.
I'm a poet – it's a funny sort of job.

HOLIDAY

I'm going away for a holiday.
I'm not sailing or going by rail.
I've found a far more cheaper way
I'm travelling by Royal Mail.

I wrote the address on my hairy chest
And stuck a big stamp on my nose.
I've tied my bags to my nice string vest
Will I get there do you suppose?

A PLOP IN THE OCEAN

Captain Copperknuckle, the grimmest and dimmest pirate ever to sail the seven seas, was in a very bad mood.

"I'm in a very bad mood!" he announced to his cowering crew through a large wooden megaphone. He took a hearty chomp from an apple and continued, spitting pips with each breath, "And I needs a-cheering up!"

The crew of the Slipperly Oyster exchanged nervous glances. They were a hardy bunch of grotty pirates but they were very scared of their captain – especially when he needed cheering up. Captain Copperknuckle was known for his fearsome temper – if ever he was unhappy (which was a lot of the time) he would simply fire the crew member. And he kept a special cannon for doing it. Belching Bessy he called her. The Captain was always asking for things. It had happened before. In fact it had happened many, many times before. Whenever they were far out at sea and the journey was very long and boring. When Captain Copperknuckle had nothing to occupy his time except shouting and eating apples he would set the crew a task and he was setting one right now. "And to cheer me up I need a gift!"

The crew groaned under their breaths.

"Is someone a-groaning?" snarled the Captain scanning his beady eye across the crew.

"Noooooooooooooooooooooo!" they all muttered back.

Captain Copperknuckle started to stride up and down the bridge. He was a short man with a long black beard that swished as he walked. He loved the sound of his own voice, but the crew didn't.

"I need something to fill my bathtub!"

All thirty members of the Slipperly Oyster crew looked up at their boss with confused looks upon their faces. It was a face they were all used to pulling whenever their captain started making his odd requests.

"I want you to find me a mermaid!"

The crew groaned once more.

"Is someone a-groaning?" snapped the Captain, hurling his apple-core over board.

"Noooooooooooooooooooooo!" they all muttered back.

That night, as the stars above twinkled their hardest to cheer up the pirates and the nightwatchman slept in the crows nest, below decks there were mutterings, mumblings and moanings.

"How is we going to get a mermaid?" hissed Polly Rodger, the girl pirate with the pink parrot.

"Where is we going to get one from?" whispered Fred Bildge, who cleaned out the toilets.

Where were they going to get a mermaid? The crew were huddled under their swinging hammocks unable to sleep a wink for worry and the threat of Belching Bessy. They huffed and puffed and hummed and ah-haaed – thinking, thinking, thinking. Suddenly from the very back of the huddled and muddled crew came a small, soft but confident voice.

"I know!"

"So do I!" said another small, soft and confident voice.

All eyes turned, like a shoal of startled fish, to the voices.
The voices were owned by the twin cabin boys, Billy and Bobby Briney. They were new to pirating and had only just joined the crew. They were still clean. Both boys were about ten and wore the same red and white striped tops with blue bell-bottom trousers.

Polly Rodger snatched a candle and stalked over to the boys. The candlelight cast wavy shadows over their faces.
"You know where to get a mermaid?" she snorted and her pink parrot curled up its beak in disbelief.
"Saw one the other day," said Billy quietly.
"Following the ship!" said Bobby, even more quietly.

Maureen and Doreen, the oceans' oldest mermaids, sat on the rudder of the Slippery Oyster combing their long grey hair and gazing at their reflections in the calm sea. The moonlight glinted off the surface of the water when suddenly Maureen squawked, "This eyeliner's running again!"
"You should try water resistant!" said Doreen, touching up her lipstick.
"Oh, what's the use? I've tried it all – bubble baths, bath salts, gels, deodorant, lipstick, lip gloss, rouge and blusher and I still can't find a man to marry!"
Doreen shrugged, "I know. I've trawled every ocean looking for someone tall, dark and handsome and can't find one anywhere. All we ever meet are unwashed pirates with grizzly beards and breath like mouldy haddock!"

At that point there was a very loud splash followed by a gurgle and a spluttering. Doreen and Maureen shrieked and looked down into the dark waters below. Something had fallen from the ship and plopped under the surface. As they gazed down suddenly a grizzly face emerged from the waves and smiled a toothless grin at the mermaids. The face and chest was that of Fred Bilge but his lower half was not what he usually carried with him. Maureen and Doreen eyed him suspiciously for the lower half of his body was made of scales and fins like that of a fish.

Maureen and Doreen clutched each other and squawked, "It's a merman!"

Suddenly, there was another splash and another splosh and another plop. From the deck of the Slipperly Oyster leapt pirate after pirate.

"It's raining mermen!" they shrieked.

A few minutes earlier Billy and Bobby Briny had made their announcement about spotting the mermaids and the pirates without a second thought (and, indeed, without a first thought) had launched themselves into action. They had decided to disguise themselves as mermen and lure the mermaids aboard and into the captain's bathtub. It seemed a simple plan, but these were simple pirates. First they set about finding disguises – and the ship had been awash with frantic scurrying and scuttling as the pirates ransacked every cubby-hole and grubby-hold for material. Fred Bilge tore his hammock from its moorings and tossed it across his tummy.

"Look!" he said, "Scales!"

Polly Rodger madly cut up a leather jerkin to make fins. Snippings flew everywhere.

One by one, each and every pirate aboard the Slipperly Oyster had thrown together a costume which could pass for a merman. Just about. Nearly.

"It's raining mermen!" shrieked Maureen and Doreen again as

pirate after pirate plopped into the bubbling blue sea and each bobbed to the surface in their makeshift disguise and swam, paddled and flapped over to the mermaids. Within minutes a gaggle of eager piratical faces were gathered at the fins of Doreen and Maureen. The faces gazed up silently.

"Hello," said Maureen nervously, "Thanks for dropping in!"

Fred Bilge was the first of the bobbing pirates to gather his wits. "We is mermen – looked at our flappy tails – and we was a-wondering whether you lovely mermaids would like to come aboard this here ship and be treated like queens!"

Maureen and Doreen looked at each and then back at the faces below them.

"We cannot stay out of water for long – we start to whither!" explained Doreen.

Fred was about to respond when Polly lurched forward plunging his head below the waves again.

"'Tis not a problem, my ladies. We have aboard this ship the finest bathtub ever to grace the ocean. There is room for at least three or four beautiful ladies of your build!"

Doreen and Maureen look at their build and thought it must be a very big bathtub, indeed. Finally Doreen said,

"Very well, haul us aboard, boys!"

It took an awful lot of rope and an awful lot of tugging to finally land the mermaids on deck, but landed they soon were and then carried flapping, flopping and giggling to the Captain's cabin and, with a mighty splosh, plopped into the his bathtub.

Now Captain Copperknuckle had been away in the land of nod whilst all this madness had occurred, dreaming of shouting a lot and eating apples. He wasn't pleased to be disturbed.

"What is all this noise, boys?" he snarled and, as he rubbed his eyes and the costumed crew came into focus, added, "And why are you dressed as fish?"

Doreen and Maureen were splashing gleefully in their new watery home. Maureen was patting the rubber duck when the Captain's words sunk in.

"Dressed?" she asked. "These mermen are not dressed as mermen!"

"They are mermen!" followed Doreen, "And hunky examples, too!" she added throwing a broad wink at Polly Rodger who gulped slightly and so did her pink parrot.

Captain Copperknuckle giggled then the giggle became a chortle and the chortle turned into a guffaw and the guffaw ended up as a hoot.

"Mermen? Them? You're walking my plank, you are! They're nothing but a pongy throng of pirates!" And the Captain laughed some more and splattered the mermaids with apple pips.

And as he laughed, one by one the pirates removed their disguises. The fins flopped to the floor and the scales fell from their knees.

Maureen and Doreen clutched each other in alarm and then screamed,. "We've been diddled!"

"Fiddled!"

"Swizzled!"

"Swindled!"

"Cheated!"

"Nobbled!"

"And conned!"

Doreen threw the rubber duck at the captain, but the ber-doing it made as it bounced off his head was lost in a tidal wave of laughter.

The next morning all was still aboard the Slippery Oyster – not a crab was stirring. All that could be heard was the occasional snore of the pirates as they slept off the effects of last night's celebration. Captain Copperknuckle had thrown open his drinks cabinet and unleashed his kazoo playing on the crew and they had slurped and burped and danced and pranced into the early hours. But now the sails were flapping in the gentle breeze, the clouds were rolling slowly by and no was awake. No one, that was, apart from two young boys. Billy and Bobby Briny. They had slept a good night's sleep, undisturbed by the goings-on that had gone on and leapt out of their hammock bright and breezy ready to face the day. But just as they were cracking open their breakfast eggs a strange noise hit their ears. It was wailing sound, a weird, whispering wailing sound. And it was irresistible. Bobby and Billy were drawn towards it as if it had enchanted them. They left their eggs sizzling in the pan and walked, almost in a trance towards the sound. Through the wooden doors of the ship, up, up the squeaky wooden steps towards the cabin of Captain Copperknuckle. And, as they drew nearer, the sound got louder and louder.

Billy and Bobby threw open the door and before them saw Doreen and Maureen lolling in the Captain's bathtub.

"Maureen's got her fin stuck in the plughole!" shouted Doreen, "And she's wailing in pain!"

"Oooooooooooooooooooooooooooooooooooo!" went Maureen.

Billy and Bobby shook their heads, broke out of their daze and into action. Bobby swiftly leapt over to Maureen and started tugging at her fin.

"It's no use!"

Billy grabbed her under the armpits and pulled and pulled and pulled until, with one final yank, she popped free.

All four let out a sigh of relief. Maureen and Doreen sat in the cold bathwater as little waves lapped their aged bodies and Bobby and Billy sat on the edge of bath wondering what to say.

"Thank you, boys!" Maureen finally said.

"But what were you doing?" asked Bobby.

"Trying to escape," Explained Maureen, "We can't spend the rest of our lives in a bath tub. We were diddled into being here. We're mermaids. We have to splash free across the ocean waves!"

Doreen added, "I told her she'd never fit down the plug hole but she wouldn't listen!"

Bobby placed his hand on Billy's shoulder and drew him to one side. They huddled together and began to whisper soft and low. Try as they might, neither Maureen nor Doreen could make out a word they were saying.

"A plan is a-hatching, Maureen. Mark my words!" said Doreen, tapping her nose.

Billy and Bobby shook hands with each other, nodded solemnly and returned.

"We've got a plan," said Billy.

"Ha! Told you!" shrieked Doreen, slapping the water and splashing Maureen.

"Like you, my brother and, I no longer wish to be aboard this boat. We are treated roughly and so, like you, we wish to be free!"

Bobby and Billy moved closer to the mermaids, looked about to make sure no one was listening and began to explain their plan.

Below decks Captain Copperknuckle was stalking the hammock room prodding the crew with his wooden leg. He had two fine sea-legs of his own, but he found this wooden leg washed up on a beach and claimed it for himself. He used it to prod his crew. Prod, prod, prod.

"Awaken, you salty sea-dogs and set about your tasks. The sail needs a-trimming, the compass needs a-boxing and my breakfast needs a-frying!"

The snoring sailors, hiccupped, snorted but failed to wake.

"So you'se refusing to awaken. Well, I think it's time for the hose-pipe, my lads!"

Back in the Captain's cabin the plan had been explained and Doreen had whipped the plug from the plug hole.

"But we'll whither, Doreen, we'll whither!" Maureen yelled.

"The boys have explained it perfectly clearly, Maureen, I do wish you'd listen!"

And Billy and Bobby Briny were on their knees spannering free the bolts that held the tub to the planks below. Turn, turn, turn. It was a tough and sweaty job, but within a few minutes, just as the final drop of water disappeared down the plug hole, the last bolt was unscrewed.

"Right!" said Billy, "Over to the window!"

And with a huge effort Billy and Bobby began inching the loaded bath tub towards the window. Its rusty legs scratching and scraping deep groves into the wood.

Maureen and Doreen giggled with delight as they gazed through the large window at the vast ocean before them.

"Break the window!" ordered Bobby.

"What with?" asked Maureen.

At that point Captain Copperknuckle, mumbling and muttering about his crew, came stomping into his cabin and threw his wooden leg on his desk with a clatter. Maureen, Doreen, Billy and Bobby froze in a pose. The captain's eyes scanned the room until they finally landed on the escaping quartet. The captain stared at the sight, rubbed his eyes and, just to make sure, stared some more.

"What in the blithing of blues blazes is you a-doing with my ba tub and why is that mermaid trying to break my window with a rubber duck?" he yelled.

Bobby and Billy quickly threw each other a nod and sprang into action. Billy grabbed the Captain's blackbeard and began twirling him around by it. In the meantime, Bobby jumped across to the desk grabbed the wooden leg and hurled it over to Maureen and Doreen.

"Break the window with this!" he commanded and they did.

Once every shard of glass has been smashed from its place a glaring, gaping hole emerged – just about the size of a bath tub.

Billy was still twirling the giddy pirate when his brother yelled, "Alright! Push!"

And Billy and Bobby pushed and pushed the bath tub towards the broken window and the open sea below.

Captain Copperknuckle clutched at his desk as his dizzying head slowed down and he just managed to grasp a final glimpse of his huge bathtub, aboard which were now Billy and Bobby as well as the mermaid, as it tottered on the edge of the window for a split second before finally plunging into the waves below.

"Whhheeeeeeeeeeeeeeeeeeeeeeeeeeeeeeee!" all four yelled as they splashed to freedom.

As the bath hit the water, they held the sides tightly until the tub righted itself and finally found its balance. Billy suddenly leaped up and slammed the plug in the plug hole.

"Plug holes can let water out and keep water in!" he shouted, "Now part two of the plan!"

And Maureen and Doreen winked at each other and slipped overboard and to the back of the tub, grabbed the sides and started pushing. Within seconds their aged flapping fins were speeding the bathtub through the water like a racing boat, slicing through the waves at a rapid rate of knots. They were heading to the sunrise, to the horizon and to freedom.

And they never looked back to see the furious face of Captain Copperknuckle poking his grizzly face through the broken cabin window shaking his wooden leg in anger, but they did hear, later that day, a loud bang followed by a long scream followed by a very distant plop.

"I think they've fired the Captain!" Billy laughed and all four slowly disappeared over the horizon.

BEEF JERKY

There once was some beef jerky
whom most thought slightly quirky
No matter the weather
would hold up a feather
and say, "Look I'm a beef jerky turkey!"

BRUNCH

The meal between breakfast and lunch
is usually referred to as brunch
but between lunch and dinner
no one eats linner
Or maybe it's simple called dunch!

BUTTER

There once was big bit of butter
who found itself all of a flutter
"Run for your life
here comes the knife
The world's biggest bit of butter cutter!"

BANGERS

A chef with a firework stash
Has cooked up something flash
His rocket salad souffle
will blow you away
and so will his bangers and mash!

CAERPHILLY

Wales is a land most hilly
Beware! Please don't be silly
Put cheese on your tyre
or you may expire,
Remember drive Caerphilly!

CHILLI

Those folk who cook with a chilli
are wrong to think that it's chilly
It really is not
It's quite freaking hot
To think otherwise would be rather silly.

EDAM

Edam is the theme of this verse
Try to imagine the word converse
For example it's true
but nobody knew
Edam is "made" in reverse.

HALLOUMi

There once was an unhappy halloumi
whose trousers were ever so roomy
"All the French fries
ran off with my size.
No wonder I'm feeling so gloomy!"

JAMBALAYA

Beware of the jambalaya
for whenever you choose to enquire
"Are you fat-free?"
replies, "Of course! Can't you see?"
He's not he's a big fat liar.

LiME

There once was a happy young lime
Who was having a wonderful time
"I've been in some sushi
played the lead in a smoothie
and now I'm the star of this rhyme!"

MANGO

A ballroom dancing mango
Once launched into a tango
But how did he feel
when he slipped on his peel
and ended up on his fandango?

SPAM

One day a thoughtful clam
said, "I know how to preserve jam,
and how to jug fish
put sand in sandwich
But please tell me how do you cure ham?

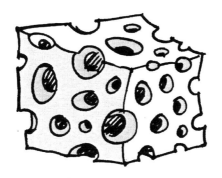

SWISS CHEESE

There once was a happy Swiss Cheese
whose holes were home to some bees
"You should see them fly
so high in the sky
Each time I do a big sneeze!"

YAM

Madam thought it quite a scam
when ordering ham, spam and spam
to shout out, "Scram!"
"But, madam", said the yam
"I simply yam what I yam!"

20TH CENTURY SOCKS

PRESENTS IN 4D
(that's one extra d!)
Contains mild stupidity throughout

Shrek Potter and the Pirates of the Jurassic Bang Bang!!

Or

Honey, I Shrunk the Smurfs

Or

Bedknobs and Scissorshands

Or

Monsters Stink

Or

PINOCCHIO: THE REVENGE!

Our story begins in the little village of Tottering on the Brink where everyone is awakening to a bubbling spring morning.

The sun was shining its most shiniest...

"Shine, shine, shine. Am I hot or what?" beams the sun.

In the trees a bluebird is gently singing, "Who let the cat out? Who? Who?"

All the village folk are going about their business.

Little Mermaid is flopping about in the horse trough – "Ooops, I think I crushed on Nemo!"

Billy Plonka is driving the garbage cart.

"Get your garbage – lots of garbage – all free today! It's scum-piddleynoxious!"

There's the usual selection of street-wise fairies and urban pixies. And Geppetto, the carpenter, is at home – ironing his false teeth – and watching "Fairyland's Got Talent!"
Simon Scowl is talking to a contestant, "So what's your name?"
"I'm Hansel!"
"And I'm Gretel!"
"And together we are – rubbish!"
"Next – what's your name?"
"Wee Willie Winky!"
Three buzzer alarms suddenly light up.
Pinocchio his son enters the room and switches off the TV.
Geppetto looks up and says, "Hi Pinocchio – gimme four! How's it going! Did you polish behind your ears this morning?"
"Daddy, there's something I have to say."
"What is it my little Pin number?"
"I don't want to be a wooden doll anymore, daddy – I want to be a real girl!"
"Pardon me?" says Geppetto. "Never, Pin, never! You're my son, I made you from bits from IKEA! There's still two legs in the box. And an ear."
"I hate you, daddy!" screams Pinocchio.
"Off to bed now, Pinocchio, otherwise your dreams will start without you!"
Pinocchio started to stomp from the room.
"Hey - Pinocchio – got your nose!"
"That's not funny, daddy!"

That night Pinocchio is in the bathroom shaving with a chisel.
"Oooh, a splinter! There's sap everywhere!"
When a cute little cricket appears on the window sill and says,

"Hi Pinocchio – don't forget always let your conscience be your guide!"
Pinocchio flicks it out of the window.
"I don't have a conscience!" he snarls.
And then Pinocchio starts to sing his "I want song"

I want some things I want them now.
I don't know what, I don't know how
Give me things, both big and small,
I want them now and I want them all!
Give me things, yes lots of things
Give those things to me!
(Oh fa-ther!!)

Pinocchio bangs down his chisel,
"That's it! From now on no more Mr. Nice Puppet!"
And he starts to sharpen his nose.

Geppetto is in bed without his teeth, without his wig and he is counting sheep when he hears footsteps coming up the corridor
Creak, creak, creak…
"Is that you, Pinocchio?"
And Pinocchio bursts into the room with his razor-sharp nose glinting in the moonlight.
"Oh, fa-ther!" he snarls.
Geppetto leaps from the bed.
"Argghh! Puppet on the loose! Puppet on the loose!"
In his panic he puts his false teeth on his head and his wig in his mouth.
"Argghhh!"
And leaps out of the window smashing the glass

He's running up the street shouting, "Help! Help!" Well actually shouting "Helf! Helf!" because of the wig.

And everyone tumbles out of their houses and chases after him. Doctor Doolittle, chatting to a slug, The Snowman is there, but it's so hot he's in a bucket. Incy-wincy-Spider Man. Little Mermaid is flopping along trying to keep up. Peter Pan is swooping over head and Tinkerbell is shouting, "Power cables!"

And Pinocchio is chasing Geppetto up the street in the moonlight towards the castle on the hill. It's a 16th century Plastic Castle – lovely red and yellow brick walls, plastic drawbridge.

It's called Castle Toisorus!

There's a flash of lightning!
FLASH!
There's a crash of thunder!
CRASH!
And they all head towards Castle Toisorus
And they arrive at the foot of the Castle Toisorus and someone says,
"Wait - that doesn't say Toisorus!"
"What does it say?"
"Toys R Us!"

And Geppetto runs up the steps to the highest turret in the castle and all the crowd are gathered at the bottom. And they chant...
"Geppetto! Geppeto! Let down your hair!"
A wig slowly floats to the ground.
And they chant, "That's not quite what we meant!"
Geppetto is on the edge of the wall, his teeth chattering (on his head) his knees knocking, his toes are huddling together for comfort when suddeny he hears,
"Oh fa-ther!"

And then it happens, doesn't it – the twinkly, tinkly music. Yes, the twinkly, tinkly music! Which means the story's about to end, something's going to change big time then we're off to get pizza. There's a shaft of ethereal light…

WHOOSH!

A choir of heavenly music

OOOH, AH, OOOH, AHH!

Glitter flitters down like heavenly dandruff.

And soon Pinocchio is cocooned in a swirling, whirling stream of light and he changes, evolves, transforms.

And then it all stops, everyone holds their breath – some hold each other's – then Pinocchio emerges from the light with glistening blonde hair, beautiful red lips and he says, "Hi, I'm Babs - can I be your friend?"

And that is the Ultimate Family Movie!

HOBBIES

I've come to a final conclusion
Hobbies are a waste of time
They only cause confusion
And mess up your leisure time.

The horse club I join dismounted
The running club just didn't start.
The maths society was discounted
And the human pyramid fell apart.

I was dropped by the parachuting club
They asked me back but refused
So I joined a bomb making club
But that was soon diffused

I was in a hairdressing club for a bit,
It was my favourite, it mattered
But they parted and finally split.
The chicken feeding club simply scattered.

The wood cutting club was whittled away
The sailing club went adrift
The Tuesday Club changed its day
I was becoming really miffed.

But the most depressing thing
That I was ever told
my favourite origami club
was going to have to fold.

DOOR

Dad took our front door
back to the DIY store.
He was angry, in a fit.
"Why bring back your door
back to our DIY store?
It's odd I have to admit."

"I brought back this door
to your DIY store,
I'm so angry I could spit,
I brought back this door
to your DIY store,
cos someone's already opened it!"

THE GREAT EXPLORER

"I am the finest specimen of human exploration,
I'll announce my next achievement with this jolly declaration
Throughout the world they all declare there's simply no one greater –
And so I announce my thrilling quest - I plan to climb the equator!

Once I've conquered that small task, I'll try something more romantic
I'll take a herd of a hundred goats and walk across the Atlantic.
I'll ski across the Sahara Desert then the mighty Red Sea I'll hike,
Followed by my greatest feat to traverse the Med on a bike

I'm planning to cross the Congo, underwater by balloon.
After that I'm going to be the first submariner on the moon
Then I'll jump off Everest with a parachute made from a map."
Then a nurse touched his shoulder and said "I think its time for your nap."

WORLD LIMERICKS

AGRA

There was a young man from Agra
who once climbed inside a jam jar
For just two quid
he'll screw down the lid
now he's a great big telly star.

BEIJING

There was a young man from Beijing
who couldn't control what he'd sing
rap, rock and roll,
funk, folk and soul
classical music and swing.

CHINA

There was a young man from China
whom most thought a bit of whiner
People hated his groans
his whinges and moans
and banished him to South Carolina.

DARJEELING

There was a young man from Darjeeling
for hours would stare at the ceiling
But had he just found
something deep and profound?
No, he's watching the wallpaper peeling.

EAST CHEAM

A young man who came from East Cheam
once swallowed some clotted cream
a pie and bananas
his tie and pyjamas
No, wait, it was all just a dream.

FROME

There was a young man from Frome
fell in love with his garden gnome
He gave it gold
and treasures untold
and declared it Emperor of Rome.

GHANA

There was a young girl from Ghana
with a highly trained piranha
it could do a fine trick
on a pogo stick
and tightrope walk across a banana.

INDONESIA

A young man from Indonesia
you've never met anyone sneezier.
His mighty blows
blew off his nose
Now he ties it on which is easier.

NANTUCKET

A sailor from deepest Nantucket
caught in a storm, but, by luck, it
wasn't so grave
he just caught a wave
now he keeps it at home in a bucket.

PENRITH

There was a young man from Penrith
who exuded a very strange whiff
But the man from Olympia
was even stinkier
I beg you don't take a sniff.

RWANDA

There was a young man from Rwanda
who was chased down the road by a panda
when pursued by bears
I have to say there's
really no need to meander.

SEATTLE

There was a farmer who came from Seattle
whose nose had a terrible rattle
He caused so much harm
as he ran through his farm
"I've scared off all of my cattle!"

TAIPEI

There was a young man from Taipei,
who, much to his wife's dismay,
one day at a wedding
made the dinner his bedding
"This is how to lay on a buffet!"

TONGA

There was a young man from Tonga
who inherited oodles of wonga
he frittered away
all of his pay
now he can't stay any longer.

TORONTO

There was a young boy from Toronto
whose mum said, "Tidy your room pronto!"
it'd caused such a distress
as it remained a mess
He said, "You see I simply don't want to!"

WHITEHAVEN

A writer who came from Whitehaven
had a head that was always clean shaven
He shaved it all day
whisked his whiskers away
Now he's known as the Bald of Avon.

A2Z
OR THE ALPHABET STORY

Have you ever wondered how the alphabet got to be in that order? A B C D etc? Why is A at the front? Why is A better than P or G, for example? Did he pay more money for a better seat? I know how letter A got to the front of the alphabet. Letter A had a really pushy mother.

"Come on Letter A!" she would shout, "I want you to be something special when you grow up!"

"Oh, mum!" A would say.

"I want you to make your mother proud!"

"Oh, mum!"

"I want to see you at the front of the alphabet!"

"The front of the alphabet?"

"Yes, the front! You don't want to end up like your father letter Z do you?"

And in the corner of the room Letter Z is slumped in a corner, fast asleep snoring. ZZZZZZZZZZZZ.

"They're doing a show called X, Y, Z Factor – get your coat!"

So Letter A went to the auditions.

"I'm Letter A. And I really believe I've got what it takes to be at the front of the alphabet!"

And main judge, Simon Scowl, said, "You really don't look like someone I could put at the front of the alphabet – you are very pointy at the top – you do know that?"

"I can work on that, Simon!" said A.

"And there's that line going across – not sure!"

"Please, Simon! I really want this!"

And in the background his pushy mother said, "Go on, Simon, make him a star!"

And Letter A went through to boot camp!
And worked and he worked.
And he finally went through to the final!
And it was down to A and B.
And B thought he was going to win because everyone love curves.
"I'm curvey!" he would say each day at rehearsals.
"And the winner of X,Y,Z Factor is."
There was huge, long pause.

About that long.
"And the winner is A!"
Huge applause! The place went mad, there was confetti every-where – Letter B burst into tears, K and L hugged each other. Letter A's mum was on her seat screaming her head off, sitting next to her is husband Z. Snoring. ZZZZZZZ

But the story doesn't end there. The entire alphabet got together to form a band and call themselves A2Z. They go on tour. Playing huge stadiums. Wembley Arena. Madison Square Gardens. They become massive. Letter A is having the time of his life. Every-where he went people asked for his autograph, which looked like this.

A

People adored A2Z. They even got their own TV show. They toured for about two years - but then things started going wrong! Arguments started! Letters wanted bigger dressing rooms than other letter. One letter smashed up his Rolls-Royce. Letters fell out with other letters. Some letters didn't speak to each for days.

Finally they called a press conference. A2Z lined up behind a long, long table.
And A said, "I can finally confirm the rumours in the press are true – A2Z is no more!"
Girls started screaming outside. Telephone lines were set-up help people cope with depression. People were interviewed about their reaction.

"I'm well-gutted!" said one
"This is the end of civilisation as we know it!" said another.
"It's terrible - I can't read a book or look at newspaper without thinking about 'em!" said a third.

And there group went their separate ways.
K, F and C left to open a chain of restaurants
B and P opened a garage.
I, T and V went into television.
M and his twin brother M start making chocolate covered peanuts
Some got a contract to appear on Countdown on Channel Four.
Q, P and R started a football club.
That was the end of A2Z. Who can forget their hot single?

a-b-c-d-e-f-g,
h-i-j-k-lmnop,
q-r-s, t-u-v
w-x-y and Z
Now I know my A,B,C's
Next time won't you sing with me!

BOUNCY CASTLE

In the bouncy castle
Lived the bouncy king and queen
And their bouncy little daughter
Princess Maureen.

They bounced all day
And most of the night
Bounced through the weekend
It was quite a sight.

But Princess Maureen
Soon got bored.
And hatched a plan
While her parents snored.

She rummaged around
And found a pin
Went to their bedroom
And bounced quietly in.

Over to the bed
With a bo-ing and hop
She pricked papa
And pop went pop

Mama woke and spoke
With a frown
"I think you've let
your father down."

"It won't happen again,
I do declare!"
Declared the princess
But that was all hot-air.

Between you and me
Her chances are blown
of ever inheriting
the bouncy throne.

KNC3000

Once, 42 scrillion light years away in that direction… ☛ there was a small planet about this big ●

It was called Planet ଊଊ and it was ruled by a mighty warrior king whose name was King Plop the 29th. There were 28 Plops before him and that's a lot of plops. King Plop thought he was the most beautiful creature on his planet. He had fifteen eyebrows, one tooth (which he kept his pocket) and a nose on the end of his finger. He had eleven legs with a spare pair for the weekend, but the most important thing about King Plop was that he loved to wear new clothes. Big clothes, little clothes, square clothes, green clothes. Clothes made of cheese, clothes made of lemonade, clothes made of tissue paper. Even clothes made out of other clothes. He loved his jelly hat, his water boots, his gravel tie and most of all his beautiful ceremonial gold pants and because he was king and he was paid 37 Dollops a day and there's 102 Wibbles in a Dollop. He spent nearly all of it on clothes.

But not far from planet ଊଊ was another planet. A horrible hideous hairy planet called Planet Eggs.

PLANET X

No, not Planet X. I said Planet Eggs! It stank of eggs and was full

114

of the naughtiest naughtiness in the whole of the universe. On this planet were two strange, extraterrestrial urchins. Two vagabonds, two rapscallions, two robbers. Their names were…

)✷■✳☀❊ …and… &⫶♦■☯♦□↗☯

Just try pronouncing those names. One day these two robbers boarded the rickety, rackety rocket for Planet ൏൏ with a dirty, devious devilish, deadly dream. That's called alliteration.

Their rickety, rackety rocket zoomed and boomed across the galaxy. Zipping and dipping and swerving and curving until they arrived with a crash at Planet ൏൏ and they climbed out and made their way to the Palace of King Plop. But it wasn't easy getting in. They were searched, they had their fingerprints taken, their toeprints taken and even had to hand in their hankies. Finally they entered the King's quarters and stood before the mighty warrior king and said:

"(▲▼□☀■✳✷)✷■✳☀❊▼)"

And the king looked at them and said, "What?"

The robbers said, "☎♦♦□☯■℔ℳ ♦❭■℔♌☯♦☽)"

"No no no!" said the King, "I meant I can't understand you. Send for the translation doughnut!" And translation doughnut was sent for and the robbers ate it in one mouthful and now all their words could be understood by King Plop.

"Your Majesty!" they said, "before your eyes, ears, nose and knees we present to you the finest spacesuit in the entire universe…"

"The entire universe?" said the King.

"Yes, the entire universe!" And they held their hands up and just as the king was about to say, "There's nothing there!" the robbers said, "Oh, one thing we must tell you - only the most high-powered intellectuals in the cosmos can see. To a fool, to an idiot, to doofus, the spacesuit is completely invisible. To someone with the brain as small as a Venusian Clam it cannot be seen!"

King Plop thought about that for a moment and remembered

how stupid Venusian Clams were. In fact, Venusian Clams are so stupid they can't even hiccup without an instruction manual.

"You don't have the brain of Venusian clam do you, your Majesty?" And the king said, "Oh, no!"

"What does your Majesty think of his new spacesuit?"

King Plop the 29th said, "I think it's fabbo! I think it's brill! I think it's well wicked! I think it is way cool etc! I love the pink gravity boots, the mauve intercom, and the lovely antennae of blue! It's the perfect thing to wear at the Plop Day Mardi Gras!"

And he paid the rotten robbers 107 Dollops each (which is a lot of Wibbles) and the robbers giggled behind their tentacles and skipped down the corridor counting their dollops.

The Plop Day Mardi Gras was held every week on Planet ෬෬ and a week on Planet ෬෬ was about the same length as a day on Planet Earth (where most of you live) so the Plop Day Mardi Gras came around very often! And was broadcast to every single TV, PC, e-phone, e-pod, and tentacle-held device in the entire universe.

Soon texts were flashing from planet to planet. Trans-galactical SMSs fizzed and whizzed through the stratosphere and words zoomed from ear to ear, nose to nose and antennae to antennae about the King's new spacesuit. Everybody wanted to see it.

The Deputy King was sent for. His name was ⟩❸◎⑤✌☜෬෬❶⍁ He was a shape shifter - and today he come as a rubber band. He looked at the clothes and twanged with excitement, "I think it's fabbo! I think it's brill! I think it is well wicked! I think it is way cool etc! I love the pink gravity boots, the mauve intercom, and the lovely antennae of green!"

"Blue!" shouted the King.

"Sorry, I meant blue!"

The Prime Minister was sent for. He was a member of the Kloop species which meant he had no bone structure, no cartilage, no inner body strengthening at all. So that's why they carried him around in a bucket!

And he saw the spacesuit and said, "I think it's fabbo! I think it's brill! I think it's well wicked! I think it is way cool etc! I love the pink gravity boots, the mauve intercom, and the lovely antennae of red!"

"Blue!" shouted the King.

"Sorry, I meant blue!"

The little strange monkey who does the king's sneezing (you don't expect the king to sneeze for myself do you?) was sent for. "I think it's fabbo! Aitchoo! I think it's brill! Aitchoo! I think it's well wicked! Aitchoo! I think it is way cool etc! Aitchoo! I love the pink gravity boots, the mauve intercom, and the lovely antennae of aitchoo brown!"

"Blue!" shouted the King.

"Sorry, I meant blue!"

The sub sub sub lieutenant was sent for, the man who folded his jam was sent for, Princess Maureen was sent for, even the King's favourite curtains were sent for and they all agreed:

"It's a perfect thing to wear at the Plop Day Mardi Gras!"

The next day the king's alarm went off with a loud splat and the king woke up and said:

"It's the day! Fetch me my spacesuit!"

Outside the palace everyone gathered. Every species, every sub-species, every mutant, every android, every half evolved life-form and a couple of cute rabbits gathered in a bubbling hub of expectation. Everyone had seen the texts, the news, the status updates, the blogs, the tweets and the telepathic newscasts and each and

117

every single one of them knew the suit of clothes was invisible to anybody with the brain of a Venusian Clam!

And no one wanted to admit to having the brain of a Venusian Clam! Would you?

So the spotlight hit the king's palace, the band of Pan-Galactic Pickle Pipers played the planet's anthem, which goes like this...

Ting!

And the palace pod bay doors opened with a **Whoosh!**

...and there stood King Plop the 29th completely naked from head to tentacle. The crowd said,

"Ooooooooooooooooo!"

and the crowd said,

"Ahhhhhhhhhhhhhhhhh!"

And other nice noises. The King paraded back and forth and forth and back in the traditional Mardi Gras fashion and the crowd chanted.

"We think it's fabbo! We think it's brill! We think it is well wicked! We think it is way cool etc! We love the pink gravity boots, the mauve intercom, and the lovely antennae of indigo mixed with violet and the merest hint of puce!"

"Blue!" shouted the King.

"Sorry, we meant blue!"

There were fireworks and cakes and music and there was fish-juggling and lettuce-spinning and everyone agreed King Plop looked fabbo, brill, well wicked, way cool etc.

Except for one small green plant with bright green leaves and bright wide eyes. He looked up at King Plop and pointed a leaf and said, "Look at King Plop!"

And everyone stopped chatting, chuckling and spinning lettuces.

"Look at King Plop!" he said again, pointing his leaf as loudly as he could.

"Look at King Plop, King Plop, King Plop!"
And a silence fell on all the mouths of all the creatures gathered for the Plop Day Mardi Gras and they listened as the small, green plant said, "He's as naked as the day he evolved!"

There was chaos!
Chaos!!

There was an explosion of coughs, mutters, splutters, splatters, zips, whooshes and clouds of dust. Everyone rushed off in opposite directions screaming, shrieking and howling with shock.
And before long the street was deserted and King Plop the 29th slowly and sadly returned to his palace, slid the door closed, sealed it and was never seen again.

And all because of one small plant who told the truth!

OTHER BOOKS

"How to Juggle Your Hiccups"
"Whelks in the Second World War"
"The Correct Way to Balance an Orange"
"I Married an Oyster"
"The Big Book of Soil"
"Hoppity, Hoppity, Hoppity, Plop"
"How to Speak Cheese"
"I Swallowed a Piano"
"The Complete History of Letter K"
"Hats for Beginners"
"Ponds: Their Place in History"
"I've Found Some String"
"Elizabeth the First and the Walrus"
(None of the above were written by Ian Billings)

There is no cheese on this page.